The Inheritance

by
Jacqueline Seewald

ISBN: 9781940758503
ePUB: 9781940758527
Mobi: 9781940758510

Cover Design: Emory Au

Published by:
Intrigue Publishing, LLC
11505 Cherry Tree Crossing Rd. #148
Cheltenham MD 20623-9998

The Inheritance

DEDICATION

This novel is dedicated to my husband, Monte, who supports me in every possible way.

Chapter One

The letter looked ordinary enough at first. Jennifer Stoddard almost tossed it in the trash, thinking it was just another solicitation. But then she noticed that the return address was in Bloomingvale, her hometown. The sender was an attorney named James Donne. The name seemed somehow familiar.

Jen opened the envelope, began reading, and sat down on the nearest chair. She was asked to contact the attorney as soon as possible in regard to her grandmother. *Velma Pritchard, now deceased.* Her grandmother, dead? It didn't seem possible. The old woman had appeared so strong both in mind and body. Could it be true? Jen bit down on her lower lip, tasting her own blood.

Her hand trembled as she pressed in the number of the attorney. An assistant answered and she explained the reason for the call.

"Please hold," the woman said.

Jen waited, tapping her fingers, annoyed by the nondescript music piped through the telephone.

"James Donne here. You are Jennifer Stoddard, Velma Pritchard's granddaughter?"

"Yes."

There was a pause at the other end. Jen felt as if she should fill it. "How long ago did my grandmother die?"

"It's been a month."

"That long ago? Why didn't anyone contact me before this? I would have wanted to come for her funeral."

"I am sorry, Mrs. Stoddard." The attorney registered what sounded like genuine regret. "We did try to phone and then write to you. No one seemed to have recent information."

Jennifer was filled with guilt and shame. "I haven't been in contact with anyone from Bloomingvale recently," she admitted.

"That is unfortunate. We did finally get your information through your mother."

Was there any point in telling this stranger about her husband's death a year ago? How much her life had changed since? But no, he would simply think she was trying to excuse her behavior—and wasn't that really the case?

"The reason I have been trying to contact you concerns the nature of your grandmother's will. It seems you are her heir. You have been left her house and savings. It will be necessary for you to come to Bloomingvale to claim them."

That came as something of a shock. "What about my mother? Isn't she the heir?"

Again, a pause. "Mrs. Stoddard, your mother and grandmother were not on the best of terms, especially in recent years as you probably know. Mrs. Pritchard felt you were the appropriate recipient of her estate. When can you arrive in Bloomingvale?"

When could she? There was Aaron to consider. "The school year ends in another week. I could come out to Bloomingvale shortly thereafter."

"Good. We'll be expecting you."

Jen replaced the receiver on her telephone and stared at it. She shook her head, trying to lose the sense of strangeness. When the doorbell rang, she didn't respond at once.

"Jen, are you there?"

She recognized her friend Maryann's voice and breathed a sigh of relief. Talking to Maryann would help her focus her thoughts. Maryann Waller bounced into the small foyer of Jen's apartment with her usual vibrant energy. Her golden hair shimmered.

"Want to go to lunch? I have some extra time."

"Sure," Jen said. "Sounds like a good idea. I have something to tell you."

Maryann raised one golden brow. "You always understate things. I get the feeling this is important."

"It could be. I guess you could say I got some surprising news."

It was June and a warm day in Manhattan but she grabbed a light jacket anyway. Many of the restaurants were overly air-conditioned and she chilled easily.

The streets were crowded with people as usual. Taxi cabs and limos honked at each other. The world around them hustled and bustled along as Maryann questioned her.

"So what happened? Someone call you with a good job offer?"

"Not yet, but then I have been out of the work world for a long time. That doesn't impress potential employers."

"Wish I could help you."

"You're in marketing. I'm a bio-chemist. They've been cutting research money, not many new drugs coming down the pipeline, less funding for development, and that means fewer jobs in my area."

Maryann let out a deep sigh. "It's true for all of pharma. A lot of the business is moving overseas."

"I may have to leave the city regardless," Jen said. "The cost of living here is very high and private school for Aaron is eating up our savings."

Jen had lived and worked in New Jersey when she first met Bill. He'd been a senior executive considerably older than herself. When they married and he'd been promoted to a vice president position in Manhattan, they bought a co-op apartment on the fashionable East Side. Jen loved the city; the excitement never grew old. There were museums to visit and Broadway shows to see.

When she became pregnant with Aaron, Bill was just as thrilled as she was. It seemed as if life could not get any better. Then two years ago, Bill was diagnosed with an inoperable brain cancer. Helplessly, she watched as her wonderful, intelligent husband lost his faculties. She prayed for a cure but none came. She lost ten pounds. Her clothes hung on her and she looked gaunt. After her husband died, Jen suffered from depression but realized she had to be strong for the sake of her son if not for herself.

Jen and Maryann decided on a deli located close-by. Jen selected a turkey club and Maryann a corned beef sandwich.

"That's a surprise," Jen said. "You usually have a salad for lunch."

"I feel like shaking things up a little today."

"That's right. Be adventurous." They shared a laugh.

Maryann certainly didn't have to worry about her figure. She could eat anything and not gain weight. She worked out almost every day at the gym in her apartment building. She was stylishly trim and always dressed in a trendy manner, usually the latest style. Maryann at twenty-seven was the epitome of a fashionable city woman. She could easily be confused for a model with her height of five feet eight inches and her striking good looks. Jen was of average height at five foot six inches. Although she happened to be just as slender as Maryann, she never thought much about being stylish. Once she'd stopped working, she felt more comfortable in casual clothing, most of the time wearing jeans and sneakers. She hadn't worked since Aaron was born. Now that he was eight years old and she no longer had a husband, it seemed that she should be working again.

"So tell me what's going on," Maryann said. She bit into her sandwich with zest.

"It's weird really," Jen said with a shrug. She picked up her own sandwich, and then put it down again. "I don't know if I ever mentioned my grandmother to you."

Maryann shook her head. "I don't remember. Maybe."

"Well, she passed away."

Maryann's great green eyes filled with sympathy. "I'm very sorry."

"So am I. Only found out about it today. Apparently, she died about a month ago."

Maryann put her own sandwich down. "And no one bothered to tell you?"

"The lawyer said they had trouble locating me. I did sell the apartment after Bill died and rent the smaller place. My grandmother broke her hip around that time. She went into a nursing care facility and I guess we kind of lost track of each other. I don't think either one of us really had it together."

"What about your mother or father? Didn't they know where you were?" Maryann took a bite of the juicy sour pickle that accompanied her sandwich.

"My parents divorced when I was seventeen and since then, I haven't had much contact with either of them. They both remarried and moved away. I stayed with my grandparents for a while after I graduated high school and until I started college in the fall. My father left town with his girlfriend. I think my grandmother was very hurt by the divorce as well as the scandal."

Maryann's eyes opened wide. "There was a scandal?"

Jen gave an uncomfortable shrug. This wasn't something she would normally discuss with other people, even a close friend like Maryann. "Well, let's just say there was a lot of gossip. They always fought a lot. When the marriage broke up, my mother blamed my grandparents for encouraging her to marry Dad. There was a lot of bitterness on her part."

"It must have been hard on you," Maryann said.

"It was. I always blamed myself, thought they were fighting because of something I'd done or said wrong. I know now it was foolish, but that's the way children think I guess. As an adult, I understand it wasn't about me." Actually, neither of her parents had ever cared much about her. When they divorced, neither one of them wanted custody of her. That was the real reason she ended up living with her grandparents the summer before college.

She would have to return to Bloomingvale, back to where her life had begun, if for no other reason than to honor the memory of the two people who had given her their love. She regretted not seeing more of them in those later years. But then everyone made mistakes, didn't they?

Chapter Two

Although she'd grown up in Bloomingvale, Jen felt like a stranger in a strange land. Many of the stores and shops appeared different. The people looked unfamiliar. She'd been raised in the heartland of America and was now back in her hometown after a good number of years. She wondered if anyone she'd known would remember her. Somehow she doubted it. She'd been quiet and shy as a child and spent most of her free time reading. Her teachers liked her much better than her peers.

She sat in the attorney's office waiting for Mr. Donne. Her appointment was set for ten a.m., but as usual she was early.

"Mrs. Stoddard." The legal assistant, Astra Meyers, according to the name plate on her desk, was staring at Jen.

"Yes. Is Mr. Donne ready to see me?"

The young woman smiled at her. "He is." With an air of efficiency, she led Jen into the lawyer's office.

Jen observed that Mr. Donne moved slowly as if his joints were arthritic. However, he took her hand and offered a firm handshake. His gaze was sharp and alert. His head moved slightly to one side as he assessed her.

"You look a lot like your grandmother," he said. She sensed some approval.

"Thank you."

He invited her to sit down on a comfortable armchair across from his desk. "It was necessary to request you come here because of the terms of your grandmother's will."

"I'm not certain I understand," Jen said.

The gray-haired attorney sat down behind his desk, steepling his hands together. "Mrs. Pritchard specified you as her sole heir. However, there are certain terms." He picked up some papers and handed them to her. "This is your copy of your grandmother's will. You will see she wanted you to have both her house and her savings."

"Yes, Mr. Donne, you told me that when you phoned." She waited as he cleared his throat.

"I'm certain you are aware that at one time your grandfather was a fairly wealthy man. Your great grandfather was a mill owner, a large employer in the area. Their house was a mansion, a showplace. Your grandmother inherited quite a lot of money and she was good at conserving it. In fact, through sagacious investing, that money continued to grow."

"She was always generous with presents," Jen said, remembering with a smile. "I don't think she ever forgot any family member's birthday or anniversary. And there were always holiday gifts as well. She was very thoughtful."

Mr. Donne gave a nod. "She was also a generous contributor to various charities."

"That doesn't surprise me."

"As I said, she wanted you to inherit her property. But there is one requirement, a stipulation. You will have to live in her house for two years or her estate will pass to charities of her choosing."

Jen stiffened in surprise. "My life is in New York now."

"That may well be. However, your grandmother was a strong-willed woman. I tried to discuss the matter with her, but she was adamant."

"I'll have to think about this," Jen said. Why had her grandmother made such a demand?

"You do that. You should know that your grandmother's wealth is well over two million dollars, perhaps considerably more. That is not counting the house which in actuality is in very poor condition and requires considerable repairs. However, a separate account has been established to pay for repairs to the home."

Jen bit down on her lower lip, her mind working furiously. "My son finished his school term. He's at sleep away camp for the next month. But after that, I suppose I could bring him out here."

"Perfect. That will give you time to start working on the house."

"Is it really in such bad shape?"

The lawyer grimaced. "Probably worse. Your grandmother hadn't lived in the house for well over a year. She was in a nursing home during that time. Her housekeeper had retired and your grandmother wouldn't trust strangers to enter. I'm afraid she let the place run down even before she broke her hip."

"Thank you for your candor." Jen had a sinking feeling in the pit of her stomach. Dealing with a decrepit old house was not something she looked forward to doing.

"It's best you understand what you'll be faced with from the start. Do you think you'll be accepting the terms of Mrs. Pritchard's will?"

Jen sat reflecting for a moment. Although she loved Manhattan, everything there reminded her of Bill. Rent for her small apartment would keep increasing as would Aaron's private school costs.

"Mr. Donne, I am going to take on the challenge and accept the terms of my grandmother's will."

The attorney got to his feet and shook her slender hand with his bony one. "I predict you won't be sorry."

Chapter Three

When Grant Coleman saw the woman start to drive through the light as it turned red, he put on his flashing lights and siren. If she'd been a local, he might have cut her some slack. But he could see by the plates that she was driving a rental. As Chief of Police, it wouldn't be right to allow some out of state driver to spit on the law. If nothing else, it set a bad example for the locals.

She turned slightly and he could see the look of surprise on her face. Pretty lady, he thought. Attractive dark auburn hair, pert nose and full lips. Too bad he had to give her a ticket, especially a moving violation that carried points. But that was how it was. He shrugged.

He indicated that she should pull over. Then he got out of his own vehicle and approached hers. "Roll down your window please, Ma'am." She did as he asked, frowning at him. "Please hand me your registration and driver's license."

"Officer, the light wasn't red when I started to go through."

"I was watching, Ma'am. It was changing before you started. You're guilty of a moving violation." He held out his hand.

Reluctantly, she handed him her information.

"Stay in the vehicle, Ma'am. Do not get out."

He went back to his cruiser and wrote out the ticket, thinking there was something familiar about the woman. When he handed the ticket to her, the woman's cheeks were flushed. She took the paper from his hand in an angry gesture, practically ripping it from his hand. She irritated him with her attitude. But instead of commenting, he gave a curt nod and walked away. He'd learned self-restraint, self-discipline and self-control in the Marine Corps. It had carried over into his civilian life and his police work. He waited at the side of the road for the woman to drive off. Mighty attractive all right but full of uppity attitude.

She was not a violent person by nature, but Jen would have liked to punch the officer in the nose. When he approached her car wearing those reflective aviator sunglasses, her heart had started to pound. The way he spoke made her feel like a criminal. He didn't recognize her and that was just as well. She was angry with herself that he could still have the same effect on her she'd felt back in high school.

As if getting a ticket wasn't bad enough, she found a dead rat on the porch in front of the door leading into her grandmother's house. Did the creature choose to take its last breath there or had some malevolent individual left the dead rat as a sign? She could think of better welcoming gifts. Either way, she saw it as a bad omen.

The white paint on the outside of the house had faded to a dull gray and black paint peeled off the shutters. Mr. Donne hadn't exaggerated the neglect of what had once been an elegant home. Her mood continued to deteriorate when she opened the door to her grandmother's house with the key that Mr. Donne had provided. What she saw made her mouth drop. If she were a Hollywood director choosing a set location for a haunted house, this would be the perfect choice.

Jen was not prepared for how dilapidated the once lovely Victorian house had become. There were dust sheets over the furnishings. The Oriental carpets were dirty and worn. Cobwebs decorated the corners of the high ceilings. There were cracks in the walls. Even the floorboards creaked with sinister glee. How could she ever bring Aaron into such a place? It must be cleaned and repaired by the time he finished camp. Mr. Donne told her he would arrange for the utilities to be turned on again, and that thought was comforting.

Then something scampered by her feet and she let out a gasp. That was it! She wasn't going to look any further, not for now. Jen hurried out to her car, sat down in the driver's seat and clicked on her cell phone, pressing the number Mr. Donne had written out for her.

After a few rings, someone picked up. "Coleman's Construction Company." A man's voice with a deep, pleasant sound.

Jen introduced herself and then explained her situation.

"Well, I can meet you at the house tomorrow morning and see what has to be done."

Jen breathed a sigh of relief. "That would be great. Are you Mr. Coleman?"

"That's right. I'm Rob. Look forward to meeting with you, Mrs. Stoddard."

She liked the sound of the man's voice. It was reassuring. Wouldn't it be nice if he were a magician? But that was only in the movies or books. She let out a deep sigh. Another Coleman. Was he related to Grant? She hoped not.

Jen decided to check into a motel she'd seen out on the highway. There was no way she could possibly stay at her grandmother's house. Strange, it had seemed so beautiful when she was young. Spending time with Grandma had been among her best childhood memories. She smiled recalling how they'd prepared chocolate chip cookies from scratch. She'd never eaten better cookies before or since. She resolved to restore the house as best she could to its former glory.

Chapter Four

The Bloomingvale Diner hadn't changed all that much over the years, although the booths were now upholstered in bright red vinyl, and the waitresses certainly appeared to be younger and more attractive than she remembered.

Jen seated herself at a booth and glanced at the menu that a pert waitress handed her.

"What can I get you to drink?" the pony-tailed girl asked.

"Iced tea would be fine."

The girl studied her with curiosity. "You're not from around here, are you?"

"I used to be."

"You talk like you're from the East."

"I suppose I lost my Midwest twang some years ago."

"We don't get many people from the East around here."

"What's good on the dinner menu?" Jen asked.

"Well, Tim, that's our cook, fixes a great meatloaf every Wednesday."

"I'm not much of a meat eater." In New York, she ate fish or vegetarian meals most of the time and occasionally chicken or turkey, but rarely if ever beef.

"We got a good chicken pot pie."

Jen shook her head. "What about a baked or broiled chicken breast?"

"Well, sure. Guess you can get that." The girl looked at her dubiously as if she'd asked for fried ants or ostrich stew.

"Thank you. Can I get a tossed salad as well?"

"What kind of dressing?"

"Oil and vinegar on the side."

"Anything else?"

"That's it." The waitress walked away to return shortly with her iced tea and a small bread basket. The bread smelled fresh and made her mouth water. She realized she'd forgotten to eat lunch.

As she buttered a slice of the thick white bread, Jen observed Grant Coleman walk into the diner and seat himself at the counter. He still had a striking presence, a charisma that set him off. Who was she kidding? The man oozed testosterone. Two waitresses practically crossed swords to see which one of them could hand him the menu first. He laughed, noting their competition.

"Now girls, I don't need quite so much attention."

"Will you have your usual Wednesday dinner, Chief?"

He gave a quick jerk of his head.

"There's garlic mashed potatoes tonight and fresh green beans."

"Sounds great. Thanks, Diane." Diane, who was also her waitress, flashed the chief a toothy smile and flounced away.

"Can I get you something cold to drink?" the second waitress asked in a voice so sweet it could have caused diabetes.

"Just ice water, Ginny."

"Right away." Ginny walked away with a wiggling movement that accentuated her rounded derriere. Could she be more obvious? Jen rolled her eyes.

Those young waitresses, probably in their early twenties, seemed intent on flirting with the local law enforcement officer. Anyone could see he was older than they were, more like thirty-four or five, her own age. Then again, hadn't she married a man several decades older than herself? Jen sighed.

The police chief turned and studied the room. His gaze narrowed as it settled on her. Jen turned and looked away. But it was too late. She found him sliding into the seat opposite her.

"Gone through any more red lights today?"

Her mouth puckered as if she'd sucked on a lemon. "None I'd tell you about."

He surprised her by laughing, a deep, honest sound. "You look familiar," he said.

"I lived around here many years ago."

He looked interested. "I don't remember any Stoddards in town."

"I was Jennifer Morrow in those days."

He gave her a steely stare and frowned. But then he extended his hand. She offered her own in return and he shook it, practically swallowing hers with his huge fist.

"I'm Grant Coleman. You and I went to high school together. We shared an English class senior year."

She studied him. He'd changed over the years, just as she had. With those sunglasses gone, she could see his gray eyes. They were the same, perceptive and penetrating. He was a mature man now but just as handsome, well over six feet tall, with a muscular build.

"I remember you very well," she said. "I'm surprised you remember me at all."

He gave her another hard look. "So what brought you back to town?"

She lowered her gaze. "You might remember my grandmother, Velma Pritchard."

He gave a nod. "I know she died not long ago."

"That was more than I knew until her attorney contacted me." Jen told him about the terms of her grandmother's will. He would probably have found out about it soon regardless, she reasoned. Small towns were that way.

Diane returned with Jen's iced tea and the ice water for the police chief. "Are you going to eat at this table?" she asked, addressing him.

Jen flushed with embarrassment. From the look the waitress turned on her, Jen understood the young woman thought she was trying to pick up the police chief. He, in turn, aware of her discomfort, stood up.

"No, I'll be eating at the counter." He turned back to Jen, picking up his glass from the table. "Good seeing you again after all this time. If you have any problems, drop by the station." With that, he left her. His words were polite but his tone was as frosty as the ice water he was now drinking. Well, what had she expected? He'd been so popular back in high school and she'd been nobody. She was surprised he remembered her at all.

For the rest of the time Jen spent in the diner, she avoided looking in Grant Coleman's direction, although it wasn't easy. Diane brought her dinner and it looked fine, but she wasn't thinking about food.

She couldn't deny it; she'd had a tremendous crush on Grant Coleman back in high school. She'd never felt such a strong attraction to another male before or since, not even Bill. But that was young love for you, so intense. A very silly, immature feeling on her part. It was a good thing he'd never known what she felt for him, or how strong her attraction had been. He probably would have laughed.

There was such a difference between them. Grant came from a poor family. His father had a bad reputation as a ne'er-do-well. But Grant didn't take after his dad. For one thing, he was an outstanding athlete. He became the quarterback of their high school football team and led them to the state title. He was a fine baseball player as well, serving as lead pitcher. His abilities didn't stop there. Grant was an excellent student. The English class they shared was an honors class for college prep students. He'd been seated next to her, and when he looked over at her and smiled, Jen felt as if the sun rose and warmed her soul. Her heart filled with joy.

Once, when she dropped her book, he'd picked it up for her. Their hands touched and she felt a surge of electricity. Their eyes met and she sensed they were somehow connected. But of course the attraction was obviously one-sided.

She'd just been fooling herself. Mr. Tall, Dark and Handsome couldn't really be interested in her. She was just a geek, a girl who had no real friends, who studied at the library and worked hard to attain high grades. He was outgoing and popular while she was an insecure loner. They had nothing in common.

They'd probably never have spoken if Mr. Owens, their senior English teacher, hadn't assigned a Shakespeare project to be done in pairs. They were to pick a scene and act it out, then explain it to the class. Hamlet provided many good scenes. Since she and Grant Coleman shared a table, they were assigned to work together.

"Where do you want to work on our scene?" he asked.

She nearly swooned. Just the sound of his deep voice was thrilling. "We could go to the library."

"We have to talk out loud. They won't like it, probably kick us out."

Jen nodded and thought about it. She didn't want to meet with Grant at his house or her own. She had no idea what his family was like. As for her mother, Sara Morrow could be very antagonistic.

"We can meet at my grandmother's house. She won't mind. She likes visitors."

And so they'd rehearsed the scene between Hamlet and Ophelia at Grandma's house. As predicted, Velma Pritchard loved the company and took to Grant. She was their audience and even applauded their efforts with enthusiasm. Jen appreciated her grandmother's encouragement.

"That was a wonderful performance," Grandma said. "The two of you make a perfect couple."

Jen had blushed, but Grant winked at Grandma and smiled.

Their presentation went well. Shy as she was, working with Grant gave Jen confidence. When the class ended, Grant walked her to the school cafeteria.

"I was thinking, would you like to go to a movie with me on Saturday night?"

Jen was thrilled and accepted eagerly. She gave Grant her home address.

Saturday evening, she fussed with her appearance as she rarely bothered to do. She set her hair, tried on one outfit after another. She asked her mother to let her know when Grant arrived.

"Stay in your room. I'll call up to you," her mother said. "A girl should never appear too eager. Boys don't like it."

But the date didn't happen. Grant never arrived. Jen cried into her pillow for most of Saturday night. Then she suffered through the worst Sunday of her life. Her father and mother had a quarrel the previous day, and he'd left Saturday afternoon not to come home.

On Monday, she wanted to ask Grant what had happened. But then she saw him flirting with Cary Barnett, the head cheerleader, blond and beautiful. They made a gorgeous couple.

When class began, he never looked her way. He even asked their teacher to change his seat to the back of the classroom. They never spoke to each other again. She felt so stupid and foolish. Of course, he hadn't meant it. She was so ordinary. He could have any girl he wanted. It was about that time Jen realized she wasn't meant to live the rest of her life in Bloomingvale.

Going to college in the East opened up her life. She remained quiet and studious, but she also became independent and gained some level of self-assurance. No, she wanted nothing to do with Grant Coleman or his ilk, then or now. Men like him only broke a woman's heart. Bill had been a fine man and a wonderful husband, perfect for her. He'd been mature, gentle and loving. She missed him terribly. Well, at least she had his son.

Diane returned, breaking into her reflections. "Is the food not to your liking?"

Jen glanced down at her plate. She'd hardly touched her meal. "It's fine. I'm just not very hungry."

"Would you like me to package it for you to have later?"

"Thank you. That's a good idea."

As she waited for the waitress to return with her bag of food, Jen couldn't help noticing how other people came over to Grant to shake his hand and say hello. He looked so good in his uniform, commanding and manly. She supposed some things never changed. Grant Coleman would always be a very attractive man, but someone she needed to stay away from.

Chapter Five

Jen didn't want to go directly back to the motel. She decided to take a walk around Bloomingvale and look at what new shops there were on Main Street and Broad. She conceded that as small towns went, Bloomingvale had a certain charm. The town had an historic inn and a village green. The library hadn't changed much either. Ivy still grew on the walls. That had been Jen's favorite place as a child with its inviting window seats. Up the street there was a bookstore, not one of the big chain stores one found in malls, but a small, friendly-looking shop.

She decided she would move from the motel to the Bloomingvale Inn, remembering how on winter days the inn served wine and cheese around a crackling fire. They also served pastries, coffee, tea and hot chocolate in the mornings. She would move into town until the house was ready. The cost would be more but it was a worthwhile indulgence.

By the time she entered her motel room and got ready to go to sleep, Jen was feeling much better. Bloomingvale might be a quiet, modest heartland town of less than 20,000 residents, but a peaceful quality abided here that one didn't find in a busy, bustling metropolis.

The following morning, after a quick breakfast of coffee and buttered roll at a fast food place on the highway, Jen drove back to her grandmother's house.

Rob Coleman showed up promptly at ten a.m. which pleased her. He was a tall man, broad-shouldered, with dark brown hair worn on the long side. He walked with a noticeable limp. When he shook her hand, Jen noted the calluses.

"Thank you for coming," she said.

"No problem. Mind if I look around before we talk?"

"Please do."

She waited while he took a tour around the premises, poking here and there. When he finished he came back and joined her in the living room that had once been the parlor.

"I guess it's in bad shape?" She licked dry lips.

He gave a quick nod. "This place will need a lot of work. Want me to write up an estimate for you?"

"Yes, I would. Mr. Donne recommended you to me. He said you do good work."

"Well, I try." He gave a modest shrug.

"How long do you think it will take to make the house livable?"

"That depends. If I work with a full crew, it won't take long. But it will cost more."

She licked her lips thoughtfully, considering her options. "I'll talk to Mr. Donne and get back to you."

He gave her a quick nod. "No problem."

"Mr. Coleman, are you related to the chief of police?"

"I am. Grant's my older brother." He studied her expression. "Hope you won't hold that against me."

She felt heat rise to her cheeks. "Not at all. I was just wondering."

She studied the man. He was well-built, muscular like his brother, although dressed more casually in jeans, T-shirt and a baseball cap. Rob Coleman's eyes were dark blue while Grant's were a piercing gray and he had a lighter complexion. Both men appeared rugged and fit.

"Don't think that just because my name's Rob I go around stealing from my clients." The half-smile informed her that he was joking. At least she hoped he was. "I won't overcharge you. I live in this town, so my reputation's important to me. I'll give you value for your money. Otherwise the police chief would arrest me."

She was saved the discomfort of a reply when her cell phone vibrated and she lifted it from her pants pocket, stared at the name that appeared and breathed a sigh of relief.

"Excuse me. I need to take this call. Why don't you work up that estimate in the meantime?"

19

As the contractor set off with his clipboard, Jen took her friend's call.

"How's it going?" Maryann asked, her voice breaking up ever so slightly.

"Not bad all things considered. I do miss both you and Aaron though." Jen licked her lips again which felt dry as dirt.

"That's what I'm phoning about. You won't have to come back to New York to pick up Aaron. I'm going to be free to bring him to you. That is if you want me to come out there." Jen heard a note of anxiety in Maryann's voice. Now what was that about?

"Want you? Of course, you're welcome here. And I would love it if you could bring Aaron out. As a matter of fact, I've decided to move to Bloomingvale. Maybe you could pack our things and have them sent out here if it wouldn't be too much trouble? I can arrange for the movers from this end."

"Wow, you don't waste any time, do you? What happened? I thought you were only going out there to find out about your grandmother's will?"

"That's the thing, if I want to inherit her estate, I have to live here for two years. I'll explain the details when you and Aaron arrive."

"Okay, I'm dying to hear all about it. What a surprise."

"For me too," she responded in a dry tone of voice. "Are you sure you want to come out here though?"

There was a hesitation on the other end.

"Maryann, are you still there?"

"I'm here all right. They let me go."

Jen was shocked. Maryann worked so hard. She was a valuable employee, devoted to her job.

"I can't believe it."

"I can. They keep downsizing. Recently, my immediate boss said he was told our department would be reorganized. I realized that meant a cut in the number of jobs."

"What will you do?"

"Take a few weeks off first. I'm entitled to my vacation time plus severance pay. Then I'll start networking, casting around for another position."

"You know I'd love to have you visit here for as long as you like." Jen tightened her grip on the cell phone. "The house is going to be fixed up. There's plenty of room for all three of us. I'll e-mail you all the details about when and where to pick Aaron up. And, Maryann, please don't tell him what I told you about the move being permanent. I really need to tell him that myself."

"Gotcha."

Jen stood in the middle of the front hall and stared off into space. Everyone thought if you worked for Big Pharma you didn't have to worry about your job. Big Pharma had deep pockets. But the times were changing. Jobs like her own in bio-chem research had been shipped to countries where the pay was low. She understood, of course. Research was expensive. Maintaining a pipeline, developing new products, could bankrupt a company, especially if the drug in development could not be approved for use due to dangerous side effects. And that happened often.

Much of their savings had been eaten up by Bill's illness, but she still had something in reserve to see her through. She wasn't certain about Maryann's situation. Her friend had obtained an M.B.A. from a prestigious but expensive university. Jen believed there were still student loans to pay off.

"Mrs. Stoddard?"

Jen looked up.

"I'm ready to discuss what needs to be done in the house. I think you better go and sit down."

Chapter Six

"It's a little dusty for sitting. Just give it to me straight. What needs to be done and how much is it going to cost?"

"Let's do a walk through."

"Okay." She noticed that he held a pen with his clipboard and wrote with a left-handed scrawl.

"This is just a preliminary estimate, you understand. I've got to do a much more thorough inspection. But this is what I see so far. First off, the roof is leaking. I might be able to repair it, patch it up temporarily, depending on the age, but chances are you're going to need a new one."

Jen frowned. "I see."

"I would like to renovate the kitchen and bathrooms, get the cracks fixed in the walls, rip away the old wallpaper and have a fresh coat of paint inside and out." His dark blue eyes met her own with directness. "I'd recommend keeping those wood floors, not replacing them. They're quality parquet. We can sand them, restore and seal them."

"Sounds good. Can you get the house ready to live in quickly?"

His look was wary. "How soon were you thinking about?"

"Like a month."

Rob Coleman let out a low whistle. "That's nearly impossible."

"Mr. Donne is holding two hundred and fifty thousand dollars for home improvement and repairs."

The man grinned. "That's a healthy budget. I can get together a crew for you and put them to work quick."

"You'll supervise?"

"I'll do more than that."

"My son and my friend will arrive in a month. So I'm going to need three bedrooms ready to use. We'll also need to be able to use the bathrooms and kitchen."

The man wrote on his clipboard. "I'll have an agreement typed up."

"Great. When can you start?"

"Things are fairly slow right now. How's tomorrow morning at 6 a.m.?"

"Perfect."

"One other thing. You'll need a cleaning crew. Do you want me to arrange for that as well?"

"Do you have a good one in mind?"

He smiled, flashing a mouthful of pearly teeth. "Sure do, the best. My mother runs it and both my sisters work for her. In fact, my mother used to clean this house for your grandmother for many years."

Jen's eyes widened. "I didn't know that."

Getting so involved with the Coleman family might not be such a good idea, and yet what were her options? She'd already agreed to using Coleman Construction as contractors for the house repair. It didn't seem very smart to offend Rob Coleman by refusing to use his mother's cleaning service.

After the contractor left, Jen wondered if she was making a series of mistakes. She hoped not. She hated making decisions and yet recently she'd been forced to make a good number of them.

"How's your dinner?" Linda Coleman asked him.

Grant watched his mother wipe her wet rough hands on her clean apron. "Fine."

"Then why aren't you eating?"

He shrugged. "Listening to what Rob's telling us."

Rob lifted a forkful of peas. "I just think Mrs. Pritchard's granddaughter coming to town is going to be good for business, though not yours, Grant. I don't think she's going to do anything criminal. But it's good for the rest of the family."

Grant shoved his plate away. "That woman is a snob."

Linda pushed back a wispy lock of graying hair from her forehead. "How can you say that? Mrs. Pritchard was for many years one of my best clients. When I was her cleaning lady, she encouraged me to expand and turn it into a real business. Now I have five employees, including Lori and Sue."

"All right," Grant conceded, "maybe the old lady was okay. But I can't say the same for her daughter or granddaughter."

"Sorry you don't like her, Grant," Rob said, "but Mrs. Stoddard seems straight to me. She didn't give me any attitude."

"Just make sure you get a tight contract."

His sisters exchanged perplexed looks. His mother frowned at him.

"Point taken," Rob gave a short nod.

Grant felt relieved when the subject dropped. He didn't want to think, let alone talk about, Jennifer Stoddard. He was glad now that he'd written her that ticket. She was prettier than he remembered. Maybe because she wore eyeglasses back in the day. She likely wore contact lenses now or maybe didn't need glasses at all.

She still had a nice shiny head of dark auburn hair, kind of wavy, not curly. Her figure was slender but not skinny. Pleasing on the eyes was the way he'd describe her. But inside where it counted, she wasn't pretty at all. He would keep that in mind. Well, he'd warned his brother and that was all he could do. If Jennifer Morrow Stoddard provided some good-paying work for his family, that was all right. He himself would have nothing to do with the woman, unless she broke the law. Then she'd better watch out.

Chapter Seven

The work on the house progressed well. Jen felt relieved that it no longer looked like something Frankenstein could have called home. Rob Coleman was a responsible worker and true to his word.

Jen couldn't help comparing Rob and Grant Coleman, even though she really didn't want to think about Grant at all. Both brothers were handsome men. She'd seen the two of them walking down the street together engrossed in conversation. Grant was the taller of the two, his build more powerful. She supposed he was a weightlifter. He looked like a force of nature to be reckoned with in his khaki summer uniform. His appearance most likely inspired confidence in the local town residents. Unlike them, she did not trust him in the slightest. She sensed his hostility toward her and couldn't for the life of her imagine the reason for it. If anything, she was the one who had every reason to harbor a grudge against him.

Thank goodness the two brothers were so different in personality. Rob was so much more agreeable. Most important, he was a hard worker. She respected that.

Two weeks before Aaron and Maryann were due to arrive, Jen consulted with Rob at her grandmother's house.

"How it's coming?" she asked.

"Oh, it's coming along all right." He flashed her a pleasant smile.

"Will the place be ready two weeks from now?"

Rob pressed his hand to his neck and rubbed it. "Don't suppose you could wait a few extra weeks before moving in?"

She had been afraid of this. "I'd rather not. Putting up my friend and son at the inn seems like an unnecessary expense when we have a house. I don't mind roughing it a bit. I take it you'll still need to be working here?"

"I won't lie to you. There's a lot still to do. But I guess we can arrange things for you and your son."

She breathed a sigh of relief. "Good. I understand things aren't going to be perfect and that you'll still be working here for a while."

She was becoming used to Bloomingvale. Residents were friendly. In the city, people generally avoided making eye contact on streets, subways and buses. That wasn't true in Bloomingvale where she was greeted with smiles and hellos from people she didn't even know.

The inn with its laid back atmosphere and old-fashioned charm was a pleasant place, and if necessary, she would stay longer, even after Aaron and Maryann arrived. But she preferred the privacy of living in a house and wished to have her own kitchen again.

One week before Maryann and Aaron were scheduled to arrive, Jen met Rob's mother. Linda Coleman arrived with her cleaning crew which included Rob's two younger sisters, Lori and Sue. Jen observed that the young women, both in their early twenties, were fairer than their brothers. Linda Coleman was heavy-set, unlike her children. Her hair was graying but she had a youthful smile and a friendly air about her. Jen immediately felt comfortable with her.

"I know this house very well," Linda told her. "My girls and I will give the place a thorough cleaning–don't you worry. Will you want us in regularly?"

Jen hesitated then said she would. There was no way she would be able to keep up a large place like this on her own. Jen decided to stay at the house and look around while they worked. She hadn't spent much time here recently. The noise of the work crew had put her on edge.

She found bookcases full of dusty volumes lining the walls in her grandfather's study. The desk and chairs were covered with ghostly white cloth. The carpet in the room hadn't been cleaned in a long time. She supposed it would take Linda and her daughters quite a long time to put the entire house to rights.

With a smile, she remembered her grandfather sitting behind his desk smoking a cigar. She'd been a small child then. But he always seemed to have time to sit her on his lap and talk to her, unlike her own father. Grandfather liked to explain things to her like how clocks worked. He answered her questions and never talked down to her. A tear formed in the corner of her eye as she reminisced.

There was a tap at the study door. "Mrs. Stoddard, are you in here?"

Jen went to the door and opened it. "Yes, I'm here, Mrs. Coleman. Do you need me?"

"One of the workers said he saw you come in here. There's a man come to see you. He was very insistent about talking to you. I invited him to wait in the living room. I hope that was all right." Linda Coleman furrowed her brow.

"That was fine. Do you know who he is?"

"I've seen him in town, but I can't say I know him."

Jen followed Mrs. Coleman into the living room. Probably many years ago it had been an elegant front parlor, a room to receive guests. She could see it already looked much better, both neater and cleaner. The furniture was now exposed, and although the chairs and sofas had become shabby, it was a big improvement over the dust covers. Coffee and end tables had also received a thorough cleaning and a coat of polish which made them shine. Mirrors and windows received their fair share of attention as well. Mrs. Coleman and her daughters had already done wonders in the brief amount of time they'd been here. Jen made a mental note to see about reupholstering the furniture rather than throwing out the chairs and sofas. The faded rose pattern wallpaper peeling in places had been removed, whisked away. Rob and his workers had painted the walls a soft eggshell that brightened the room considerably.

The gentleman seated on a straight back chair rose to take her hand. His digits felt damp and limp. She removed her own hand as quickly as possible. She studied him. His bespectacled face was round. He was plump and balding. What hair he did have reminded her of snow. She judged him to be in his late fifties or early sixties. He wore a dark-colored suit, white shirt and blue stripped tie which seemed a bit formal and conservative given the warm weather.

"I'm Samuel Forrest," he said. He spoke as if she should know who he was.

"Were you a friend of my grandmother?" she asked.

"I would like to think we were friends." His smile was benign.

"I'm sure you know that she's deceased."

His gaze saddened. "Yes, I was aware of that fact. She was a lovely woman, and most generous. She'll be greatly missed."

Jen waited.

"Your grandmother was a large contributor to the charity I represent. I visited often and we had many good talks."

"What charity are you connected with?" Jen asked. That seemed to be the response Mr. Forrest expected.

"I am the Director of The Forrest Foundation. It's an international organization that feeds and supports starving orphans throughout the world."

"That sounds very worthy."

"Oh it is indeed." Mr. Forrest removed his eyeglasses and wiped them with a handkerchief he took from his jacket pocket.

"I am hoping you can take up where your grandmother left off. As I said, she was an extremely generous benefactor."

Jen was starting to feel uncomfortable. "Right at this time, Mr. Forrest, I'm not in a position to make any large donations. My funds are rather limited."

Samuel Forrest's smile did not reach his eyes which bore into her. "Your grandmother was a wealthy woman, well-invested. As I understand it, you've inherited her estate."

This really wasn't any of the man's business. She frowned in annoyance. "Sir, my inheritance really doesn't concern you. Now please excuse me for now. I have matters that need my immediate attention."

"Of course," he said, his tone of voice cold enough to freeze ice in January.

Jen hoped she hadn't been rude, but there was something about the man she didn't like or trust. She saw him to the door and was relieved when he had gone.

"Mrs. Stoddard." Linda Coleman bustled into the room followed by her two daughters. "Unless there's something you need done right away, we're finished for now." She waited expectantly.

Jen went and got her wallet from her handbag which she'd left out in the kitchen and paid Mrs. Coleman. "You've done a lovely job. I'll call you to come back soon to continue cleaning."

Rob and his crew did wonders renovating the kitchen. He also arranged for a new stove, refrigerator and dishwasher to be installed along with granite flooring and new counters. She would use the old-fashioned kitchen and dining room furniture for the time being, she decided. There was a solid, homey feel about them.

The next few days were hectic for Jen. She did a lot of shopping for the house, storing basics and groceries, whatever she thought might be needed soon. As promised, the things from her apartment arrived. Beds and bedding were set up in the three bedrooms that Jen intended to use. The kitchen had to be organized as well. She spent time with Linda Coleman and her daughters, examining the pots and pans in the pantry, seeing what should be kept and what tossed. She found the mother and sisters were hard workers with cheerful dispositions. Good down-to-earth women whose company she appreciated.

Things were going well. She'd been worried about being ready on time for her son and Maryann's arrival, but it seemed that it would happen as planned. Jen breathed a deep sigh of relief.

One day before she planned to drive out and pick up Maryann and Aaron at the airport, Jen worked in the house giving special attention to the living room. She'd discovered her grandmother's Wedgwood miniatures that had always sat on the large marble mantle over the fireplace. They'd been wrapped up and tucked away in a corner of the front hall closet. Jen smiled, remembering how much Grandma had loved her knick-knacks. She was giving them a thorough cleaning when the front doorbell rang. She knew it wasn't any of Rob's crew. Today they were busy painting the outside of the house. Maybe a neighbor was dropping by. She still felt shy with strangers but had to admit it would be nice to know some of the neighbors.

When Jen answered the door, she discovered her mother and a man she did not recognize staring at her. She blinked to make certain this was not a mirage.

"Don't just stand there with your mouth hanging open. Invite me in." Her mother's nostrils flared.

"Of course, please come inside."

"Not that I should need to be invited into my own mother's house. This is Frank, by the way."

Jen glanced at the stranger. He in turn looked her up and down in a way she didn't much like. His hair and mustache were salt and pepper. His body wasn't fat but he did have a mid-section that protruded over his pants.

"Why don't you come out to the kitchen and I'll fix you some lemonade or iced tea."

"I'll sit down in the parlor. You can bring the drinks out here to us."

Jen recognized what her mother was doing. "Can I ask why you're here?"

"Don't I have every right?" Sara fluffed her dyed red hair like a matador waving a cape.

"Where's your husband, Mother?"

"Oh, him. He's my ex. Frank is the man in my life now, aren't you, honey?" She patted the man's hand.

Frank grunted his agreement.

"I'll bring you those drinks," Jen said. "Why don't you get comfortable in the living room?"

Jen needed time to pull her thoughts together. She and Sara hadn't seen each other in six years. So why had her mother come here now? Clearly, it wasn't for a mother daughter reunion. Jen fixed the iced tea, poured it into three glasses, found a box of packaged chocolate chip cookies and carried it all out on a tray. She set down the tray on the coffee table in the living room.

"Please help yourselves," she said.

"Aren't you the good hostess." Her mother's painted lips dripped sarcasm.

Jen waited. She knew Sara would get to the point of her visit soon enough. She didn't have long enough to take more than one sip of her beverage.

"So when do I get my share of the inheritance?"

"I don't think Mr. Donne mentioned Grandmother leaving you anything. Did he contact you?" She managed to keep her tone of voice neutral.

"Yeah, I flew in for the funeral. More than I can say for you." An accusing long blood red fingernail pointed in Jen's direction.

"I didn't know." Jen lowered her eyes.

"Well, you should have kept in touch. Anyway, I want what's due me."

"Mother, I have nothing to do with the terms of Grandma's will. You really have to take that up with Mr. Donne, not me."

"I'll just bet I do." Sara puckered her lips as if she'd been sucking on a lemon.

"In any case, I don't get a penny unless I live here for two years. So I have nothing to offer you."

"Fine. We'll just see about that. I'll be back. Don't think I won't. You'll be sorry if you don't do what's right by me." Her mother's gaze was as menacing as her threatening tone of voice.

After Sara and Frank slammed out of the house, Jen sat on her chair for several minutes, too stunned to move.

Linda Coleman entered the room with a dust cloth in her hand. "Did I see your mother?"

"I'm afraid so."

Linda flashed her a warm smile. "Mrs. Stoddard, your mother always did have a sharp tongue on her. Sorry, I couldn't help overhearing. Don't let her get to you."

Jen found tears had formed in her eyes. "Thank you, Linda. Please call me Jen. I appreciate your support."

"You're going to find that there are lots of good people in this town, ones who'll want to know you if you'll give them the chance."

"I hope you're right."

"Oh, I know I am." Linda Coleman touched her shoulder.

Jen couldn't help comparing Linda's family to her own. Except for Grant, they were kind-hearted and friendly. Well, her grandparents had been fine people too, in her opinion. Maybe Bloomingvale was the right place for her.

Chapter Eight

Late that afternoon as Jen left the house and started to drive away, departing for the inn, a strange sound whizzed across the open front car windows from the driver's side through the passenger side. She was startled by the sound. Her heart began to pound. Jen glanced over at the thicket of overgrown shrubs and trees to the side of the grounds that led back into woodlands. Had the sound been a bullet? If so, it had nearly hit her. Her hands shook on the driver's wheel as she took off at high speed.

One block away she heard the police siren and saw the flashing lights. She groaned. Not again! He signaled with his hand, pointing his index finger for her to pull over. It was all she could do not to burst into tears.

Grant Coleman approached the car like a gunfighter in a spaghetti western. "I thought you learned something the first time," he said. "Guess I was wrong. License and registration." He held out his hand with a bored, impatient gesture.

"I have a very good reason for speeding."

The smile was more of a smirk. "I've heard them all, but you can try."

"As I left my grandmother's house, a bullet passed through my car. I had the windows rolled down. So they weren't broken, but it just missed hitting me."

He stared at her. "Maybe it was a kid with a BB gun. Are you certain it was a bullet breezing by you? How familiar are you with weapons?"

"Not familiar at all, but I know what I heard." Jen swallowed hard.

He let out a loud laugh. "In Bloomingvale? I doubt that very much."

"So you're not taking this seriously?" She folded her arms over her chest.

"Admit it. You're just looking for an excuse to keep me from writing you another ticket." His intense gray eyes bore into her like the steel blade of a dagger.

Jen raised her chin and stiffened her spine. "You are so wrong. Why don't you check the area near the house, just to see if you can find anything?"

"Waste of time." He leaned toward her and she felt his breath on her cheek which caused her to shiver. "Tell you what I will do though. I won't write you a ticket this time because that's the most creative excuse I've ever heard."

"So glad I managed to amuse you," she said.

Jen watched him drive off. He was probably still laughing, the sexy jerk. Several people had come out of their houses and were staring at her. Jen managed to restart her car and drove off before others gathered. She certainly didn't want to make a spectacle of herself. Letting out a shaky breath, Jen wasn't certain now if she'd really heard what she thought she had. A professional law enforcement officer didn't think anything of it. She supposed it might have been nothing at all. Maybe it was a child with a BB gun as he suggested. But try as hard as she might, Jen couldn't convince herself.

"Mommy!" Aaron saw her waiting and ran into Jen's arms.

She hugged her son and held him to her. "I missed you so much."

She ran her hand over his hair that was as a newly minted copper penny. Jen loved the little boy scent of him. In truth, she loved everything about him. She tried to kiss him, but he pushed her away.

"Kissing is yucky. It's for little kids. I'm big."

Jen smiled. "Yes, you are. How did you enjoy camp?"

"It was cool. Me and my friend Josh caught a frog. We had to let it go though. Our counselor said it would die if we kept him. So we set it free."

"That was good. Creatures are meant to live in the wild not in captivity."

Maryann stepped forward and hugged her. "Aaron and I enjoyed the plane ride, didn't we?"

"Yeah, it was an excellent adventure."

"Did you see lots of planes at the airport?"

"Lots and lots. They took off and they landed. So cool!" Aaron's face was pink and beaming, showing the kind of enthusiasm only a child could experience.

Jen smiled. "We're going to have another adventure. My grandmother left me her house and we're going to live in it."

Suddenly the smile faded from Aaron's face. "For how long?"

"Well, it might be for a long time. We'll have to see."

"Okay, as long as we get back in time for school."

Maryann looked at Jen, her green eyes enlarging. Jen knew exactly what her friend was thinking. Selling Aaron on remaining in Bloomingvale might be a real challenge. Jen wished she had Maryann's marketing skills.

Jen drove them past Main Street with all its charming shops, the brick casements filled with flowers and plants at this time of the year, adding considerable beauty.

"Very nice," Maryann said. "Don't you think it's pretty here?" She turned to Aaron.

"It's okay, I guess." His small shoulders rose in a noncommittal shrug.

"We started fixing up the house," Jen said. "I think you're going to like it. There's a lot to explore. The workmen are still around. You can watch what they're doing."

Aaron seemed to perk up. "Okay, that could be fun."

"You bet it will," Maryann said with a big smile and gave Aaron a thumbs up.

Chapter Nine

The month of August had become hot and humid. They didn't call these the dog days for no reason. Add to that the house wasn't air-conditioned and she, Maryann and Aaron were all uncomfortable. Jen made a mental note to discuss this situation with Rob Coleman.

"I really would like central air throughout the house," she told Rob when he arrived at the house.

"So would I," Maryann said. "It's positively sweltering."

"You have an idea how much it would cost?" Rob scowled.

"A lot?"

Rob gave a quick nod. "Got that right. More than you can afford right now. The house was built long before there were such things as air-conditioners let alone central air. The wiring and duct work alone are major jobs. Tell you what I could do, put in a more powerful attic fan for the time being. Also, we could put window units in the bedrooms, kitchen and parlor area. How would that be?"

"Thanks, Rob. That will help a lot."

Maryann eyeballed the good-looking man working in her friend's house. She liked what she saw. Rob Coleman had a broad back and shoulders and well-muscled biceps. Ordinarily, she didn't pay much attention to construction workers, but he was different. You could tell a lot about a man from the way he treated children, and Rob was very good with Aaron.

"Can I help you work?" Aaron asked Rob.

"Sure you can. I can always use a good helper, as long as your mom doesn't object."

The man had patience and answered the boy's questions without being rude or patronizing. Maryann really did like that. She even liked the dimple that winked in his right cheek and his deep baritone voice.

After Jen left them to run some errands, Maryann turned her attention on Rob Coleman.

"So have you lived here all your life?"

"Except for serving in the military." He gave her the full extent of his smile which she had to admit was something to behold. "You always been a big city gal?"

"No, I lived in Connecticut originally. But I took my M.B.A. at Fordham in New York. I did an internship in Manhattan and have been working there ever since."

"Good credentials."

"Oh, I don't know. It didn't seem enough to impress my employers. They downsized my department."

"Tough break. So you're between jobs?"

"For the time being I'm taking advantage of Jen's hospitality."

"Well, there's plenty of room in this big old house."

"I guess when it was built, people had large families."

"Suppose so." He wiped his sweating brow with the back of his hand.

"Would you like something to drink?"

"You can leave a pitcher of something cold outside for us workers to drink. Seems like it'll be real hot today."

She tried to ignore the fact that he topped her by a good several inches and very few men of her acquaintance did. He was all lean, hard muscle. She wasn't looking for a summer fling, but if she were, Rob Coleman would fit the bill very well indeed.

"Are you working on the roof today?"

"We sure are. We'll try to see if we can patch it, but I think it's going to need replacing."

"I suppose there are lots of leaks in old houses like this one."

He gave a nod.

That morning, Maryann brought out several pitchers of lemonade and placed them on the redwood table out back.

Around eleven-thirty, as she sat at her laptop by the kitchen table updating her resume, Rob Coleman returned.

"We'll be chopping down some of the hedges," he said.

"Don't do it until you've talked to Jen. You should get her approval first. She took Aaron over to the elementary school this morning. I'm certain they'll be returning soon."

He stepped forward so close that she felt his warm breath on her cheek. He wiped his sweating face with the back of his large, callused hand. She studied him thoroughly. He was a few years older than she was. But he gave a young impression. Broad-shouldered and powerful, dressed as he was in faded jeans and work shirt, if one looked only at the work-hardened body, he could easily pass for twenty. But there were lines etched in the weather-beaten face. He had strong features, and his eyes were a clear dark blue.

"Those thorny bushes have got to go. They're murdering us."

"I'm certain Jen won't mind, but you do have to ask her permission."

He smiled at her showing even white teeth. "Haven't you heard the saying it's easier to ask forgiveness than permission?"

He went back out and her eyes followed his departing body. She let out a deep sigh. Time to get back to working on her resume. Must not lose perspective. Best to avoid distractions. Getting another job was number one on her to do list.

Chapter Ten

"Why did we have to visit the school here? I don't understand. Aren't we going back home at the end of the summer?" Aaron's voice was practically a whine. His eyes narrowed.

Jen gently touched his shoulder. "Let's get a treat at the bakery and then we'll talk about it, okay?"

Aaron's mood immediately improved. Jen didn't intend to bribe her son with food, but a little bit of sugar made the medicine go down a lot better.

The woman working behind the counter at the bakery had snowy hair. She might have been elderly, but her hazel eyes sparkled.

"You always had the best chocolate cream donuts."

"We still do. Would you like one?"

"Why don't you make it a dozen donuts and give us a variety?" Jen was thinking of Maryann, Rob Coleman, and his crew.

"My pleasure," the woman said with a big smile. "And what would you like, young man?"

Aaron looked around the displayed pastries with eyes larger than his stomach. "That one." He pointed to a chocolate cupcake with coconut frosting.

"My favorite too." The woman's pronouncement was delivered with a wide smile.

Jen studied the donuts. "Those Boston crèmes look yummy and what kind of jelly donuts do you have?"

"We baked apricot and blueberry for today." The woman pointed to them in the display case.

"A half dozen of those would be great."

After handing Aaron his treat, the woman boxed the donuts and handed them to Jen.

"I like this place," Aaron said sniffing the air. "It smells good here."

"We agree," Jen said with a smile.

"You seem familiar," the woman said, turning her head to one side.

"I used to live in town a long time ago. I was Jennifer Morrow then. My grandmother recently passed away and I'm living in her house now. Her name was Velma Pritchard."

The woman extended her hand. "I'm Aggie Bigelow. You might say this bakery is something of a landmark in Bloomingvale, been a family business for over a hundred years. I knew your grandmother and your grandfather too. Good folks. You be sure to come back again often. We bake fresh bread and rolls every day."

"We'll definitely be back, Mrs. Bigelow," Jen said.

She paid for the purchases, and took the box of goodies into her hands. Then she led Aaron to the town square which had numerous benches beneath large shade trees. They sat down together and Jen watched Aaron wolf down his cupcake.

"This is really good, Mom. Aren't you going to eat one too?"

"A little later, sweetheart. Back at the house so they can be shared. There's some things we need to talk about. I thought it might be good to discuss them between us in private."

"You mean without Maryann?" He gave her a questioning look.

"Or anyone else. Yes, just you and me."

Aaron finished gobbling down his cupcake and Jen automatically handed him a napkin. She waited while he wiped his mouth. He threw her an impish grin and she thought what a good-natured child Aaron was, and how much he reminded her of his father.

"Honey, when I was a child, I saw a pair of shoes in a store window. I fell in love with those shoes and wanted them so badly. They were shiny patent leather just perfect for parties. I asked my grandmother and she offered to buy them for me as a birthday present. When we went to the store, they didn't have them in my size and I was terribly disappointed."

Aaron nodded solemnly. "They couldn't order the shoes for you?"

"No, there were no others. But the gentleman who owned the shoe store told me that although the shoes looked pretty, they were actually not very comfortable. He brought out another pair of shoes, not as pretty but very comfortable. You know what? They became my favorites. The point I'm trying to make is that we don't always get what we want but sometimes what we do get is really good, maybe even better. We just need to keep an open mind. We don't always know what's really best for us. Does that make any sense to you?"

Aaron turned his head from side to side. "I guess." His dark brown eyes, so like her own, appeared thoughtful. He dangled his feet over the green bench and stared at the grass beneath.

"We're going to be living in my grandmother's house for at least two years. The house is a gift from her to us."

Aaron got to his feet. "But we live in New York. We don't live here."

"This is a good place. It's where I grew up. I think we could be happy here."

Aaron's chin trembled. "My friends aren't here."

"You can make new friends."

Jen tried to place her hand on her son's small shoulder but he shrugged her away.

"I don't want to stay here." She could tell that further discussion at this time would be pointless. Aaron's chest heaved and he looked ready to burst into tears.

"I have to take these pastries back to the house before they melt in the heat." Jen could see the idea of moving to Bloomingvale had taken Aaron by surprise. She decided to beat a strategic retreat for now. She bit down on her lower lip wondering if he would come around. If not, she would be faced with some hard choices.

Chapter Eleven

Rob Coleman entered the house through the kitchen door. "Could you get us another pitcher of something cold right away. It's hot as Hades on that roof today. You'll find some corpses if you don't keep the water coming."

"I was just about to do that," Maryann said. "Great minds think alike."

She noted that he was red-faced, perspiring profusely, proof the heat was taking its toll.

"We're back." Jen and Aaron entered the kitchen.

Maryann saw that Jen was carrying a bakery box. "Something tasty?"

"You got it. I think we all deserve a break."

"Guess you're right about that," Rob said as he watched Jen untie the string holding the box together. "I'll tell the guys to climb down. "I can take some of these outside to that old picnic table."

"You're welcome to stay here," Jen said.

"We're pretty grubby. Outside's fine. There's shade in the yard."

Aaron approached Rob in a shy manner. "Can I come out later and watch you work?"

"Sure you can, sport. Better still, I have some work to do inside too. You can be my helper, that is if your mom doesn't mind."

All eyes turned to Jen. "No, that would be fine." Jen turned to her son. "Why don't you change into old clothes so you'll be able to help Mr. Coleman when he's ready?"

"Cool!" Aaron ran out of the room.

Maryann smiled. "You're really good with kids. Do you have some of your own?"

"Nope, not married." Maryann straightened her posture. So this very attractive man was a bachelor. How interesting. "I like kids, that is, as long as they don't try to move my ladder when I'm working on a roof."

"Oh, Aaron would never do that," Jen said.

"Glad to hear it." Rob winked at Jen.

"Think I'll go up and change to work clothes myself." Maryann thought Jen looked tired.

"How'd it go at the school? Did you register Aaron for the fall?"

"I have to arrange for his records to be sent." Maryann saw worry lines appear around Jen's mouth and forehead.

"Didn't Aaron seem to like the school?"

Jen frowned. "I don't think so. He doesn't understand why we're not going back to New York. He likes his old school and he has friends there."

"Maybe I could talk to him."

"Do you think it might help?"

"It's possible. I have two younger sisters and I could usually convince them to do things they didn't much like. Some people think I have a way of connecting with folks. I'll have a go at it while we work together later. Maybe I can talk him around."

"Rob, thank you so much. I appreciate your help." Jen left the room.

Maryann turned to the man. "That was a really nice thing to say."

Rob shrugged. "It's no big deal."

"You're a good guy, Mr. Coleman and a very handsome one as well."

He flashed a smile at her. "Are you flirting with the hired help?"

"Technically, I didn't hire you. And yes, I guess I am flirting with you just a little. Do you mind?"

He drew closer to her. "I could think of worse things than having a pretty green-eyed blonde warming up the room."

"Maybe you better have some of this lemonade. I wouldn't want you getting too warm."

A look passed between them, and it did intensify the heat in the kitchen. At that moment, three sweaty men descended on the room.

"Guys, we're taking a break outside in the shade." They took the pitcher, glasses and box of pastries.

Maryann grabbed a chocolate donut before they made off with all of them. She caught Rob Coleman giving her a long, considering look before he left the kitchen. She smiled to herself and took a big bite out of her pastry. Chocolate had never tasted quite so sweet.

Chapter Twelve

Grant saw his brother sitting at the counter in the diner and decided to join him. Rob was mopping up soft boiled eggs with a slice of white toast.

"That looks good," Grant said.

Rob gave him a nod. "It is."

Grant snatched a home fry from Rob's plate.

"Hey, order your own food." Rob smacked his hand away.

"I intend to." Grant favored his brother with a broad grin and chewed the purloined fry with gusto.

"You cops can't be trusted." Rob narrowed his eyes.

"Funny, I've heard the same thing said about contractors."

Diane approached them, ponytail swinging. "Chief, what can I get for you?"

"Eggs scrambled easy, wheat toast, O.J. and coffee."

"Have it for you in a few." She gave him a big, wide smile. Then she set him up with coffee and refilled Rob's cup.

As the waitress sauntered away with Grant's order, Rob turned to him. "She really likes you. Thought about dating her?"

Grant shook his head. "Too young for me. Besides, I'm not that interested in dating."

Rob eyed him. "You let the divorce with Cary sour you."

Grant stared down at his coffee cup. "Cary acted like she was crazy in love with me. Didn't take long once I was deployed for her to latch on to another guy. She didn't take her marriage vows seriously."

"Women aren't all like Cary. She always seemed kind of flighty. You were a real popular guy and she was head cheerleader. So she latched on to you."

"When I blew out my knee in college and gave up on trying for pro football, I wasn't quite so appealing anymore."

"If you ask me, you and her got married too young." Rob finished his food and pushed the plate away. "Doesn't mean there's not some terrific woman out there who'd really love you."

"Like I said, I'm never letting any woman make a fool of me again."

Rob gave him a hard look. "It's not just what happened with Cary, is it?"

Grant stared up at the grease stained ceiling of the diner.

"What happened with Mom and Dad? Right?"

Grant shifted in his seat.

"I hate talking about our old man. You know that. He's dead. It's over. Best forgotten."

Rob pulled him around by the forearm so that they were facing each other. "The thing is it's not over so long as what happened in the past is affecting the present."

"This isn't the time or place for talking about family matters."

Rob gave a nod. "All right. But we need to discuss it sometime."

"I'm not so sure of that."

Diane returned with the coffee pot and topped off their cups much to Grant's relief. The conversation with Rob had taken a bitter turn. Some things were best buried and unsaid.

Jen watered the thirsty shrubs that lined the drive. The house was coming along nicely thanks to Rob and his crew. She hoped by the time they finished there would be enough money left over to give each of them a bonus. Rob and his workers had painted the front of the house and restored some of its previous glory. New black shutters smartened the white exterior. She was pleased with the results. Gardening was called for as well. She made a mental note to ask Rob about that. She felt certain he'd know someone reliable.

"Hello there."

Jen looked up. A woman a few years older stared at her. She was wearing a straw hat and sunglasses, had dark wavy hair and a well-endowed figure. The woman removed her sunglasses and continued to watch Jen with curious eyes. Jen shut down the hose.

"Are you the one everybody's talking about?"

"I'm Jennifer Stoddard. I'm not aware that people are talking about me."

The woman held out her hand. "Maggie Higgins. Sometimes referred to as Magpie. And in small towns, people do gossip. There's often not much else to do."

"I don't doubt it if they're finding me a person of interest."

"Good answer."

"I'm planning on living here for a while. Actually, I lived here for a while when I was younger. I wouldn't mind knowing some of the neighbors."

"We live just up the road from you."

"Mom!" Aaron came running toward her. "Guess what? I just beat Maryann at checkers."

Maryann came up right behind him. "Hey, short stuff, I think you cheated."

"Did not!" Aaron stamped his right foot down and folded his hands over his chest.

Maggie smiled at Aaron. "I have a boy about your age."

"You do?" Aaron blinked, listening with attention.

"I have a daughter too, but she's older. I have a feeling my son Bobby would like to play checkers with you."

"Awesome. There's no other kids around here." He lowered his head.

"You'll meet plenty of kids when you go to school."

Jen noticed the look Aaron tossed in her direction. The mention of going to school in Bloomingvale clearly upset him.

"We're having a barbecue on Saturday afternoon. My husband Eric loves cooking outdoors. We invite friends, family and neighbors during the summer. Would you like to come? It would be a chance for you to get acquainted with some of the local people that live in town."

Aaron turned pleading eyes on her. "Can we, Mom?"

"Of course." She turned to Maggie Higgins. "We will be delighted to attend. Thank you for the invitation. What would you like us to bring?"

"Just yourselves." Maggie Higgins glanced at her watch. "I better get going. My walking time is about over. If it wasn't so hot, I'd try jogging back." Maggie provided Jen with her address and then took off.

"What did you think?" Jen asked.

"I like her," Aaron replied. "She seems nice."

"I think she's nice too," Maryann agreed. "You're a good judge of character, Aaron, even if you do cheat at checkers."

"Sore loser."

"Come on. Give me a rematch. Bet I beat you this time."

Chapter Thirteen

Saturday turned out to be sunny and blessedly less humid. Jen started going through her clothes trying to decide what to wear. Was she expected to dress up? Not for a barbecue. Would jeans and a casual short-sleeved shirt be appropriate? It would have to be.

A loud knock sounded at her bedroom door "Are you busy?" Maryann walked into the room.

"I was just trying to figure out what to wear. You know I can't remember the last time anyone invited me to a party."

Maryann's green eyes were bright. "Don't start getting nervous. It's just a small town get-together. No big thing."

"I'd like to make a good impression on these people. I'm going to be living here for at least two years. I want to fit in for Aaron's sake."

"Sure, I understand." Maryann sat down on the bed and kicked off her shoes.

"I can't figure out what to wear."

"Want me to loan you a sundress?"

"Like the one you're wearing?" Maryann's sunflower dress was form-fitting and flattered her curves.

"I know what you're thinking. You're so transparent. Forgive me for saying this, Jen, but you're awfully conservative. You need to dress up a little. Let me help you."

"What do you have in mind?"

"I have a sports dress that would look great on you. Simple cut, demure, classic lines. Honor bright." Maryann held up her hand in a Girl Scout pose that made Jen laugh.

"Okay, I'll try it on."

"Great." Maryann bounced off the bed. "And after we fit the dress on you, I'll help with hair and make-up."

"Maryann, you know I hardly ever wear any make-up."

Her friend turned around at the door. "Yes, I know. But you definitely need some. At least a little eyeliner, mascara and lipstick. Nothing major."

Jen shook her head. "Nothing major?"

They decided to walk to the Higgins home rather than drive. It was only half a mile up the road. The Higgins family lived in a spacious old Victorian not all that different from her grandmother's house. But it was very well maintained. A large porch with comfortable wicker chairs welcomed them. They were about to walk up the front stairs when someone called to them to walk to the back of the house. Sure enough they could hear the buzz of conversation before they arrived.

Maggie Higgins came around to greet them. She'd dressed in navy shorts and a dressy pink T-shirt.

"So glad you could make it," she said. "I'll introduce you to everyone. But first, Aaron I want you to meet Bobby." She glanced around and then called out to a boy half a head taller than Aaron. He came over with a wide grin on his face.

"Aaron, this is Bobby. He's going into third grade."

"So am I," Aaron said.

"I got a cool new game for my birthday. Want to see it?"

"Sure." The two boys took off together chattering as if they'd known each other all their lives. Jen couldn't have been more pleased.

"Usually Aaron's shy with new people, but he's really taking to your son."

"Bobby's outgoing like me. Now I promised to introduce you both to the town people." Maggie hooked one hand through her arm and the other through Maryann's. Jen felt as if she were a character in The Wizard of Oz.

First they were introduced to Eric Higgins, Maggie's husband. Apparently, he worked as a veterinarian.

"What kind of animals do you care for?" Maryann asked.

"Mostly big animals, cows, horses. But we work with dogs and cats as well. I don't believe in discriminating."

Jen saw he had strong forearms. He was well-muscled and tall, fair as his wife was dark.

"Eric, you remember Velma Pritchard, don't you?"

"Sure, I do. She was something of a philanthropist. Donated money to our animal shelter."

"Well, Jennifer is Velma's granddaughter."

Maggie's husband shook Jen's hand enthusiastically.

Maggie next brought them over to meet a local doctor. He put down his cold drink and shook Jen's hand. A trim middle-aged man, he spoke in a pleasant voice. He had graying hair and a ruddy complexion.

"Dr. Gus works with his daughter, Ella."

She and Maryann shook hands with Ella and the doctor's wife, Abby Kramer.

"I couldn't ask for a better partner in the practice than Ella," the doctor told them. He placed his arm proudly around his daughter."

Maggie explained that Jen was Velma Pritchard's granddaughter. The doctor's face lit up.

"Your grandmother was a wonderful woman. I was her doctor for a number of years. Couldn't ask for a better patient."

"Did you visit her in the nursing home?"

"Certainly did."

Jen worried her lower lip. "Did she die suddenly or were you expecting it to happen?"

Dr. Kramer gave her a sympathetic look. "Your grandmother was elderly. I had expected her to recover. She was feisty. Still she was frail. They phoned me from the nursing home. There was nothing I could do for her. She lay in her bed looking as if she was asleep. Her heart must have given out. A fine lady and never one to complain about anything. Always had a positive attitude even when she was in pain."

Jen lowered her eyes, feeling both grief and guilt. She should have phoned more often, at least that. But she had been in such a dark place herself. Still, that was no excuse.

Next, Maggie introduced them to a local dentist, Noah Winthrop, who also welcomed them. It seemed he was a bachelor and looked both Maryann and herself over with interest. He gave them a large, toothy grin.

Maryann whispered to her as they walked away to meet yet another town resident. "Did you see that mouthful of capped teeth? He's a walking advertisement for his wares." She giggled.

Jen shushed her friend. "I hope I can manage to remember everyone's name."

Maggie turned to her. "It'll probably take a while."

"I've got nearly a photographic memory. I'll remember for both of us." Maryann waved a bee away as it buzzed at her.

"Good, because I want to introduce you both to Mayor Longworth. She's a good person to know."

The mayor was a woman, plain in appearance, mousy brown hair cut brutally short, wearing black culottes with a white sailor blouse. She gave them each a firm handshake.

"Nice to have new people in town," she said in an authoritative voice.

"Nice to meet you too," Jen said.

Maggie pulled them along. "Now I'll introduce you to our police chief."

"Oh, no, that's not necessary." Jen stopped moving.

"Yes, it is." Maggie dragged her on.

Then Maggie tapped Grant Coleman's arm, causing him to turn around and face them. Jen saw he'd been in conversation with his mother, brother and sisters.

When Maggie tried to introduce them to the Colemans, Grant stopped her cold.

"We're already acquainted."

"Then I'll just leave you to chat for a while. Eric is signaling me. I need to put out more salad platters and help him with the burgers." She hurried off before Jen could say a word.

"So Mrs. Stoddard, run any stop signs today?"

She felt herself flush.

"Now Grant, don't tease her," Linda said, placing a restraining hand on her son's forearm.

"Who says I was teasing?" Grant lifted one dark brow.

"We walked here today."

"Glad to hear it."

Maryann lifted her chin. "Jen's a very careful driver. But she might be a little rusty. There's not much call for driving in the city. Manhattan's too congested for it to be practical to keep a car available. Much easier to take public transportation or cabs. Of course, if you're well-to-do there's always car service or limos."

"Different world, I guess," Rob Coleman observed.

"It is that," Maryann agreed.

"Can I get you ladies a cold drink?" Rob asked

"Sure, I'll come along with you," Maryann said.

Jen was left standing there with Grant Coleman, his mother and sisters. She felt awkward and couldn't think of a single thing to say to them.

"Rob mentioned the house is coming along nicely." Linda said.

"You'll come in next week. See what you think."

"We'll have to delay it and come the week after," Lori said. "We have a full schedule next week. Sorry. Mom was planning to let you know tomorrow."

"No problem. That'll be fine." Jen looked from Lori to Sue. "You two wouldn't happen to be twins?"

Sue smiled. "We are, but we're fraternal not identical. Most people don't guess we're twins. I got my father's light brown hair and blue eyes. Lori has Mom's darker coloring."

"Eric's putting out burgers," Linda said.

"I'm starving," Lori said.

Linda and Sue followed close behind. That left Jen standing with Grant. She looked down at the grass.

"So Mrs. Stoddard, am I making you uncomfortable?"

She looked up and met his eyes for the first time. They made her think of silver bullets. Well, he wasn't the Lone Ranger, now was he?

"As I said to your mother, please call me Jen."

"Is that to prove how democratic you are, just folks like the rest of us?"

"I don't appreciate your sarcasm. What did I ever do to deserve it?"

"Excuse me," he said, "I need to check in with the station." He whipped his cell phone from his pocket and hurried off.

The man was outright rude. She could think of nothing she'd ever done to incur his hostility. If anything, she'd given employment to his entire family. She was the one who ought to be angry at him, not the other way around. What was going on in that thick skull of his? He might be the most physically attractive man she'd ever laid eyes on but he had no manners whatsoever.

Chapter Fourteen

Maryann didn't remember the last time she'd found any man quite so appealing. She and Rob Coleman had walked off together and stood in a semi-private spot beneath the shade of a large elm tree.

"A quarter for your thoughts," he said.

"That's pretty steep."

"Inflation." He shrugged, the dimple forming in his cheek.

"I was thinking how friendly people are around here."

He gave a quick nod. "It's a good town all right. A decent place to live and raise children. We all want to make it even better. Get more people to visit, buy our goods and services. You're in that kind of field, aren't you?"

"Yes, I work in marketing. That's the area of my MBA."

"You'd be a real asset to this town."

Maryann shook her head. "I'm not staying, just visiting with Jen this month and helping her get settled in."

He took a swallow of the water bottle he held. "Too bad."

"What could I possibly do around here? I'm used to working for a big corporation. I'm a product marketing manager."

"Is that how you know Mrs. Stoddard?"

Maryann took a drink of diet soda from the plastic cup she held. "Actually I knew her husband Bill before I knew Jen. He introduced us. I interned at the company. He was my boss, a vice president. He recommended me for my job."

"What happened to him?"

Maryann lowered her eyes. "He died of a brain tumor. It was awful. He was really a great guy. Jen and Aaron suffered a lot. That's why I'd like to see them happy here. Jen's a wonderful friend. I can tell your brother doesn't like her. But he's made up his mind without knowing her. I think he's really unfair."

Rob Coleman shook his head. "My brother's a good man. He cares about people."

Maryann dropped her cup into a nearby garbage bin and placed her hands on her hips. "Well, sure, I'd expect you to say your brother's okay."

He placed his hand on hers and she felt a frisson of electricity. She quickly withdrew her hand but wondered if he'd felt something similar when they touched.

"The thing you have to understand about Grant is that he's the oldest of the four of us." Rob looked around as if to make certain no one stood nearby able to listen in on their conversation. "Our father was good at fixing things and did all kinds of repairs for a living. But he drank." Rob lowered his voice further. Maryann moved closer.

"When the old man drank, he wouldn't just pass out the way some drunks do, and he didn't act silly either. He got mean. My mother hated him drinking, wanted him to quit. Mom would eventually lose her temper with him and they'd fight."

Maryann swallowed hard. "You mean argue or physically fight?"

"Both. He put her in the hospital a couple of times. But she wouldn't press charges. Said it was just as much her fault as his. Well, Grant didn't see it that way. As he got older, he tried to stop them from fighting. So the old man turned on him and beat him up. Grant hated him. I remember Grant telling him he wished Dad would die. That was right before the old man drove off drunk and wrapped himself around a utility pole."

Maryann's eyes opened wide. "How horrible."

"Yeah, it sure was. Grant's a good guy. But he's complicated. He took more abuse than the rest of us. And he was sensitive about coming from a poor family. Got himself a football scholarship to college. Injuries stopped him from having a pro career. But he went into the Marines as an officer. He served with honor. And now he does an outstanding job as police chief."

"What about you Rob? Did you serve in the military as well?"

He gave a nod.

"And is that how you hurt your leg?"

"A gimpy foot seems like a small price to pay for surviving. I still got a leg to stand on and I'm grateful for it. We served our country, Grant and me. I'm proud of the fact."

"Of course, you should be."

"Tell me a little about yourself."

"I'm originally from Connecticut. My dad's an engineer and my mother teaches foreign languages, French and Spanish to be exact. I'm twenty-seven years old and I've worked in the business world since I was twenty-one. I got my graduate degree evenings while I worked days. I suppose you could say I'm highly motivated."

Rob cocked one eyebrow. "Why is that?"

"I guess I always felt in competition with my older brother. Hank and I weren't close growing up. He was seven years older than I was, and my parents' pride and joy. They adored him."

"But you evened the playing field. Right?"

She shrugged. "Not exactly. Hank's a neurosurgeon, one of the best in the country."

"Maryann, if you're not happy in New York City, why not look for a way out of the rat race?"

She shook her head. "I'm a city girl, Rob. It's all I know how to be. And I do love the culture, the theatre, the opera, ballet, museums. They're all there. Fine restaurants. The city's alive day and night. Here they roll up the sidewalks after it gets dark."

"Now you're exaggerating. I'm going to prove to you that this town is a great place to live and work."

"Is that a challenge?"

"You bet it is." He gave her a broad grin.

"Fine. I like a good challenge." She lifted her eyebrows.

"It means you're going to be spending a lot of time with me."

"Am I?" She gave him a teasing, flirty smile and he loved it.

"We're going to be joined together like Siamese twins whenever I'm not working."

She lifted her chin in a confrontational pose. "Are we now?"

"Think you can handle it?"

"I'm tougher than I look."

Chapter Fifteen

While Aaron was enjoying the morning visiting with the Higgins family, Jen decided to look at cars at the dealership out on the highway.

She drove the rental with Maryann as passenger. It felt good getting away from working on the house. Around them the flat farmland stretched out on both sides bursting with growing crops, cradling them in its bountiful fertility.

"Inspiring, isn't it, seeing all of this?"

Maryann glanced around. "I'll say. What a contrast to the city."

Jen glanced at her friend sideways. "I saw you and Rob Coleman looking very cozy at the barbecue."

Maryann shrugged. "Don't go trying to act like a matchmaker, Jen. You know I'm going back to New York after Labor Day weekend. I really need to get a new job."

"There might be something for you around here."

"Yeah, like maybe the diner will need an extra waitress?"

"Just saying, you can never tell. With life, anything is possible."

"When did you get so optimistic?"

"I'm just being selfish. I hate to see you leave."

Jen took a deep breath. "So what do you think I should say to the car salesman?"

"Tell him what you're looking for. Don't talk price. Let him tell you. I'll let him know whatever he's asking is too much."

"Are you sure it will be?"

"Of course, it will. Honestly Jen, sometimes you're a tad naïve. They always jack the price higher for women."

They were almost at the dealership when Jen saw a truck slow down ahead of them. She put her foot on the brake pedal, pressed down, and it went to the floor. Nothing happening. Jen began to feel sick to her stomach.

"Oh, no!"

Maryann turned to her. "What's wrong?"

"The brakes are gone."

"My God, Jen, look out! We're going to smash into the back of that truck."

Jen did her best not to panic. Her heart hammered. Her mind raced. "I can turn into those fields off the side of the road." She pulled the wheel sharply, veered into a corn field and then yanked up the emergency brake.

They came to a jerky stop, the car covered with vegetation. Maryann had called for emergency assistance before Jen finished catching her breath.

"Glad the airbags didn't blow up," Jen said. Her heart still pounded. "What now?"

"I guess we wait for the police to come. The car rental company will demand a full report."

The police weren't long in coming. Who should get out of the patrol car with a uniform officer falling in stride right beside him, none other than Chief Grant Coleman. Jen let out a groan.

Chapter Sixteen

Grant Coleman threw her a knowing look as he approached the car. Then he shook his head. "We have to stop meeting like this."

"Not very funny or original." Jen frowned at him.

"I think you need a refresher course in driving, Mrs. Stoddard."

Maryann came toward him, hands fisted at her hips. "That is so unfair! Jen is an excellent driver, careful and mature. The brakes went out on the rental. That's certainly not her fault."

"All right, ladies, call the rental company. If they approve, we'll have the car towed to Stuart's, that's our local garage in town. Dave Stuart is a first-rate mechanic. He'll see to the car and let us know what's going on. Meantime, can I offer you transportation back to town?"

Jen cleared her throat. "Actually we were driving to the car dealership just a few miles up the road when the brakes failed. I need to buy a vehicle of my own and return the rental."

"Okay, I'll drive you over there if you're up for it." He strode back to his cruiser expecting them to follow.

Maryann raised her eyebrows as they exchanged a look.

"We both have cell phones, Chief. We can request a cab."

"Why bother? I'll save you the trouble."

"Fine, I'll just get my handbag." Jen went back into the rental car and retrieved her pocketbook. Maryann did the same.

"I might be able to help you work a deal on a car. I know a fella works there, salesman by the name of Art Garrison."

"That won't be necessary. I don't want to take advantage of you, Chief. I'm certain you have much more important things to do with your time."

He gave a quick nod. His expression was distant, giving nothing away, but Jen had a feeling that she'd offended him. They rode in uncomfortable silence. She was grateful when Grant Coleman pulled into the dealership's lot. Pick-ups were most prominent on the lot.

"Thank you for taking us here," Jen said, hoping she sounded polite as well as appreciative.

"Anytime, Mrs. Stoddard. We public servants aim to be helpful to the public."

"Chief, please call me Jen. Everyone does. There's no need to be so formal."

He placed his hand to his square jaw as if contemplating something. "And here I thought all you high class rich people frowned on familiarity with us lesser folks."

"I don't understand." She wanted to ask what his problem was but realized being hostile or confrontational wouldn't get her anywhere with this man.

"Jen? Ready?" Maryann asked.

Jen nodded and they entered the showroom. They were instantly hit by a blast of arctic air. Jen wished she'd brought her summer jacket. She shivered. A salesman dressed in a gray business suit, striped blue tie and white shirt approached them. The smile showed a mouth full of teeth like a shark. He appeared to be a few years older than she was and had something of a beer belly.

"What can I help you with today, ladies?"

"We're interested in purchasing a new car," Maryann said. "My friend has moved back to Bloomingvale and needs family transportation."

The salesman gave them a steady look and then extended his hand, shook first Maryann's hand and then Jen's. "My name's Chuck. I'd like to help you choose a fine automobile. We have a terrific selection. Do you see anything on the floor that interests you?"

"I'm not certain."

"Well, why don't you have a look around, see if there's anything you like, and then we can talk."

She and Maryann walked slowly around the showroom looking at the cars on display and their price range.

"I'm not looking for anything expensive," she said softly to Maryann. "The thing is I feel pressured now because we don't have the rental."

"I know. It's a real problem."

"I think I'd like to look at some of the used cars on your lot," she told the salesman.

"Sure thing."

Finally, they chose a car Jen felt she could afford. The salesman tried to talk them into a number of extras which Jen refused. He also wouldn't come down on the price. Jen began to perspire in spite of the chilled air.

Then she heard a familiar voice. "Art, I want to introduce you to Mrs. Stoddard. She's come back to Bloomingvale to live and she needs a reliable car."

She turned. "Chief, I thought you'd left."

"I did, but thought I should come back and check on you."

"I'm not your responsibility."

"Well aware of that." He leaned negligently back against a fire engine red car, his muscular arms crossed in front of him. "Art here is the manager of Garrison's. His dad owns the place."

Chuck looked from Grant Coleman to Arthur Garrison. "I've been helping this lady and her friend, but Art if you'd like to take over negotiations, that's fine with me."

"I'll see you get the commission," Garrison said. He had a deep, gravelly voice and like Grant Coleman was a tall imposing man.

Chuck walked away.

"Art, can you give Mrs. Stoddard a good deal on one of your cars?" Grant looked relaxed and in his element.

"Don't see why not." Art Garrison turned to her. "Which car catches your fancy?"

Jen told him and sure enough he offered her a much better deal than Chuck had.

After Jen had signed the paper work, she left the showroom in something of a daze. By that time, Grant Coleman was long gone. It felt like a relief that she wouldn't have to thank him for his help.

Chapter Seventeen

"That was twice today the police chief came to your rescue," Maryann observed as they stopped to pick up groceries before heading back to the house. "He is a strange man. I mean he acts as though he dislikes you, and then goes out of his way to be helpful."

"I don't comprehend him any better than you do." Jen parked the car and got out.

Maryann followed her. She gave Jen a speculative look. "Maybe his feelings are different than what we thought."

Jen gave an uncomfortable shrug. "I don't think so. He does seem complicated though."

After Jen took a cart, Maryann followed her. She looked at the store with interest. "This is a pretty cool store. Reminds me of the bodegas in the city."

"DeNuccio's Market is another one of the shops that's been here forever. It's a family owned business like Bigelow's Bakery, and they take pride in providing quality."

Maryann examined strawberries and then peaches. "These are good. Best I've seen in a long time. Is all the produce like this?"

"It is. Kind of spoils you for the supermarkets." They loaded up on produce and then took a look at the fish counter.

"Now this isn't as good as New York, but it will have to do I suppose." Maryann wrinkled her nose.

"I think beef and poultry are the strong suits here. There's no Fulton's Fish Market and no nearby ocean. You have to consider that."

"Not a problem. We'll manage. I like fruits and vegetables better anyway."

"Across the street next to the post office you'll see an Italian restaurant."

Maryann peered through the front window. "The Red Pepper? Interesting name for a restaurant."

"Best pizza in the heartland."

Maryann laughed. "Which means it doesn't measure up to Manhattan."

Jen faced her friend. "That's not what I mean. One of the DeNucci children opened The Red Pepper back when I was in school. They do great Italian food. Everything fresh. All ingredients bought right here at DeNucci's. We'll have to eat there soon. You'll see."

"And here I thought they offered nothing but a diner in this dinky town."

"Well, the diner's really popular too. But for a special meal, you can't beat The Red Pepper. It's jammed in the evenings."

Maryann sniffed as they got into the automobile again. "I think they spray the inside of a resale to give it a new car smell." Maryann leaned back against the bucket seat.

"I hardly noticed. I'm not all that comfortable driving the car yet." She found her hands were holding tight on the steering wheel.

"You'll get used to it." Maryann gave her an encouraging smile.

"I hope so." Jen couldn't forget how the brakes had failed on the rental car. It had been downright terrifying. They could have been in a bad accident—or worse. She gripped the steering wheel until her hands began to sweat.

Chapter Eighteen

They had just finished a light dinner consisting of pasta and salad when the doorbell rang.

"I'll get it!" As usual, Aaron ran rather than walked to the front door.

"Wish I had his energy," Maryann said as she helped clear the plates.

"Funny, I wish I had yours," Jen responded.

Moments later, Rob Coleman followed Aaron into the kitchen.

"Good evening," he said, "hope I'm not disturbing anything."

"We just finished dinner," Jen said.

"Rob, you can come up to my room. I got this cool game," Aaron said excitedly.

The contractor looked down at his sneakers. "I'd like to do that, sport. But maybe another time? I came by to ask Maryann if she'd like to step out with me this evening."

Maryann's mouth opened in surprise. "This is a bit sudden. Why didn't you phone?"

Rob shrugged. "Didn't have your number. Didn't want to bother Mrs. Stoddard since it wasn't about business."

Jen smiled. Rob actually looked embarrassed. She surmised he'd acted on the spur of the moment and was now looking for excuses.

"Why don't the two of you take off for a while? Aaron is going to help me with the cleanup."

Aaron groaned. "Mom, do I have to?"

"You do."

Maryann turned to Rob. "Where do you want to go?"

"I was thinking of bowling. There's a good place just one town from here. Serve good nachos too."

Maryann screwed up her features. "I haven't bowled since high school. Even then I wasn't very good at it."

"I could teach you. It's a friendly, fun game around here."

"Can I go?" Aaron asked.

"Next time," Jen told him.

"I'll go change," Maryann said.

"You look fine," Rob said.

"Pretty spiffy yourself," Jen commented and watched Rob's cheeks turn pink.

"Spiffy?" Maryann repeated with an arched brown.

"One of my grandmother's expressions," Jen said.

"I must remember to add it to my vocabulary." Maryann turned to Rob. "Okay, let's go."

Jen watched them leave and smiled. Maryann and Rob made a nice couple in her opinion.

Chapter Nineteen

The doorbell rang for the second time that evening. She'd just gotten Aaron tucked in for the night and wasn't expecting anyone to come by.

The doorbell rang again as if the person ringing the bell was impatient.

"Who is it?"

"Grant Coleman."

She hesitated but then sighed and opened the door. "I thought it might be the big bad wolf come to blow my house down."

He didn't smile. In fact, his expression looked downright grim. He had a shadow of beard and in the overhead hall light his face appeared as all hard angles and planes. The police chief gave the impression of a force to be reckoned with, formidable and strong as granite.

He strode into the house not waiting to be invited in. "Can we talk in private?"

"Aaron's asleep and Maryann is out with your brother."

His square jaw came up in an expression of surprise. "I didn't know they were dating."

"It wasn't that formal. He just came by this evening and asked her out. Why don't you take a seat in the living room? Can I offer you something to drink? Tea, coffee, lemonade?"

"Nothing. This isn't a social call."

She gave him a sharp look. "Somehow I didn't think it would be."

He followed her into the parlor and took a straight back chair. She seated herself on the farther sofa and waited.

"Dave Stuart's a really good mechanic. He's also a friend. Since I was the one making the request, he looked at your rental right away." He paused.

"And?"

"He says someone tampered with the brakes."

She stood up, her heart racing. "I didn't expect that."

He got to his feet as well. "Neither did I."

He began to pace the room.

"Couldn't it have been an accident?"

"Dave claims the line was cut in such a way as to let the brake fluid drip out slowly which would mean you would likely be on the road when you lost your brakes."

Jen sat down heavily feeling suddenly weary. "Was someone trying to kill me?"

"I don't know about that. There are lots better ways if that was the intent. Might have been some sort of a warning."

"Like the shots that went through my car?"

He ran his right hand through his thick brown black head of hair. "Yeah, as to that. I did do a check after speaking to Dave. I found shell casings."

"Not BB gun pellets?"

"They came from a rifle."

Jen placed her hands over her heart. "I just can't believe it. Somebody actually wants me dead."

He turned then and came toward her. "Not necessarily. It could be someone wanting to frighten you."

"But why? I haven't hurt anyone." Jen didn't realize she was crying until the tears began rolling down her cheeks. Then she was sobbing.

It was just too much. She had lost her husband and tried to carry on as best she could. And now this. Her whole body shook with the force of her sorrow. Strong arms came around to hold her. She tried to pull away, only to find her legs like rubber. Do not let me faint, not in front of this man! But she was dizzy and the world momentarily became lopsided and dark, spinning out of control.

It's all right," he said, cradling her in his arms as one would hold a small child. "You'll be fine." His voice was soft and soothing. His arms were tightly around her, as she pressed her face against his hard, muscular chest. One hand stroked her hair.

"Y-you can let me go now," she told him in a breathy voice.

"Certainly." But he didn't let her go right away; he just kept holding her against him with his strong hands.

"Really, I'm all right," she told him, straightening, stiffening her spine.

But he still didn't let go of her. Instead he brushed his lips over hers. She sighed and he deepened the kiss. She slid her arms around his neck, letting her body melt against him, returning his kiss with hunger and passion. In his arms she felt safe, protected by the heat and strength of his powerful body.

Then he pulled away.

"I'm sorry. I shouldn't have done that," he said.

She wasn't certain what to say, how to respond. There weren't any words that seemed right.

They sat down again, separate and apart, she on the sofa, he on the straight back chair.

"Why did you kiss me?" she asked in a breathy voice.

He shook his head. "Damned if I know. Why did you respond?"

"I couldn't say." She studied the worn Oriental rug.

"Are you aware of anyone who might wish you harm?" She looked up. He was the cop again, cool and professional. His gray eyes were sharp as a steel sword and just as probing.

"I can't think of anyone. I really don't have any enemies."

"Mrs. Stoddard, clearly there is someone who wishes you ill."

She looked up. "Please call me Jen. I'm tired of the formality."

He paused a moment as if considering. "All right, Jen, is there anyone who's got a grudge against you?"

She bit down on her lower lip, remembering the unkind words her mother had expressed, the bitterness toward her. But surely not! Sara Morrow was her mother. Then again, she had a new boyfriend. Jen hadn't forgotten the nasty leer he'd sent in her direction. But that couldn't be a reason to try and harm someone. She was confused and it must have shown in her facial expression.

"Come on, Jen, tell me what you're thinking."

She shook her head, not wanting to discuss the matter. But in the end, she broke down and told him. He listened without interrupting. Finally, when she was done, he spoke.

"You think your mother might be out for revenge because your grandmother by-passed her on the inheritance?"

Jen leaned forward, running her fingers through her wavy auburn hair. "I don't know. She seemed really angry and she's never been what you'd call warm or loving like mothers are supposed to be. She said hurtful things when I was a child. But to actually try to physically harm me? It's not her style."

"What about this boyfriend of hers?"

"Frank." She shrugged. "I don't know anything about him. He struck me as slimy, but that's just an impression."

"Okay, I'll take it from here." He started to leave. She followed after him.

"Wait. There could be someone else."

He turned and gave her an intense look. "Like who?"

"I don't exactly know. But Mr. Donne, my grandmother's lawyer, he might be of some help. He knows all the terms of her will. I'll phone him in the morning."

"Good. Set the appointment. We'll see him together."

"And you won't talk to my mother until we've seen Mr. Donne?"

He gave an abrupt nod. Jen felt a sense of relief. The thought of Grant Coleman confronting her mother was distressing. If her mother had nothing to do with what happened, then everything would just be that much worse between them. No, it was best to talk to the lawyer again and get his input and insights into the situation.

After Grant left, Jen locked up. She set the outside light on the front porch for Maryann and then went upstairs. She was exhausted and just wanted to lie down and rest. The thought that someone had deliberately set out to harm her was upsetting. It seemed to her that Bloomingvale had many lovely residents. Yet could one of them or maybe her own mother be behind this? What a horrible thought! Jen wouldn't allow herself to think about it until tomorrow. She'd had enough for one day. As for Grant Coleman, she found him disturbing as well.

Chapter Twenty

Maryann observed that Jen, considerate as ever, had left the porch and entry hall lights on. She turned on a lamp in the living room and then made her way to the kitchen. She realized Jen and Aaron must be sound asleep by now. That was fine. She wanted, needed some alone time. She decided to put on the tea kettle, found a chamomile tea bag, and fixed herself a cup of the soothing beverage. As she blew on her cup of tea, Maryann realized she was more than a little bemused. Rob Coleman had that effect on her.

What should she make of the man? For one thing, he was a lot more intelligent than outward appearance would suggest. If she were honest with herself, she'd admit to being attracted to him on all levels. But the relationship, if she could even call it that, wasn't destined to go anywhere. He needed a woman who'd settle down in Bloomingvale. Sure it happened to be a very nice Middle American town, but it wasn't New York. The city vibrated with excitement and high energy. Here life moved at a slow pace, everything low key. Bloomingvale offered no challenges as far as she could see.

So why had she agreed to see Rob again outside of the confines of Jen's house? Why had she given him her cell number? Providing mixed signals wasn't her style. She prided herself on being honest and forthright in her dealings with other people. She must tell Rob she wouldn't see him socially again. Yet even as she made the decision, she felt a stab of pain as if a knife had pierced her heart. She wished he didn't appeal to her so strongly.

There was a smashing sound. She jumped to her feet realizing that a window had been shattered. Vandalism in small town America? Well, it could occur anywhere. Probably some teenager being a jerk.

Maryann hurried to the study where the sound had originated. Sure enough a window had been broken. A large rock with a paper rubber-banded about it lay among the shards. She carefully picked up the rock trying not to cut her hands on the shattered glass. Should she look at the paper? Maybe save it for the morning and show it to Jen. She certainly wasn't going to wake her friend up just to upset her. But Maryann felt troubled. She prided herself on having good instincts and intuition. Something was off here and didn't bode well for her friend.

Chapter Twenty-One

"What does the paper say?" Rob stared at the rock Maryann had left on the desk the previous night.

Jen shook her head. "I didn't read it yet." She stared at it as if it were a rattle snake ready to strike. "I called you because we need the window repaired."

"Sure, that's not a problem." Rob rubbed his chin, looking thoughtful. "But you need more than a window repair. I'd like to call my brother and mention it. Might be nothing but a kid's prank. Then again, maybe not. Let's see what Grant thinks."

Jen felt her face flush. "I've bothered him enough."

Maryann placed her hand on Jen's shoulder. "Rob's right. I think you better call him. He is the police chief."

Jen's mouth was dry as cotton. "You heard Rob. It's probably just a kid's prank."

She really didn't want to be in contact with Grant Coleman so soon again. At best the situation felt awkward to her. But Rob took it out of her hands. He used his cell phone and called his brother.

"Morning. You have time to come out to the Pritchard house? There's something I think you need to have a look at. Thanks."

Grant Coleman arrived at ten a.m., put on a pair of plastic gloves, and viewed the paper that had been bound to the rock.

"Who handled this?"

"I picked it up from the floor," Maryann said. "I heard the glass shatter and came to check out what happened. But I didn't do anything else, just placed it on the desk."

"Okay, not a problem." Grant freed the paper from the rubber band and examined it carefully. After reading the written words, he frowned.

Jen's heart lurched. "What does it say?"

Grant held up the paper so they could all see it.

Jen read it out loud. "Leave town or you'll be dead."

She turned to Grant. "What do you make of it?"

"Kid prank, right?" Rob said.

Grant shook his head. "Can't say for certain." He pointed to the lettering. "These words have been cut out from the local newspaper. The paper itself is common stuff. My guess is there won't be any fingerprints to be found other than Ms. Waller's. I think something more is going on here."

Jen placed her hand over her chest. Grant saw the gesture and touched her shoulder.

"Mrs. Stoddard, Jen, I don't mean to upset you, but we need to take the incident seriously."

"What's the matter, Mom? Why did someone throw a rock through our window?" Aaron scrunched his small face into a look of worry.

"It's really nothing, sweetheart. Let's go to the kitchen and leave Rob and his brother to fix things. Okay? Maybe I will bake those muffins after all. You can help me. Maryann, will you help too?"

"Sure thing." Maryann looked from Rob to Grant.

"We'll bake enough for everyone." Jen took her son's hand and Maryann walked beside them.

Aaron withdrew his hand and skipped along beside her. Jen waited until they entered the kitchen to speak again.

"Aaron, could you go upstairs and change to shorts and a T-shirt? We don't want to make a mess of your pajamas."

"Sure. But don't start without me."

"We won't."

He bounded from the room like Tigger. She waited until she was certain her son was out of earshot.

"I didn't get to tell you. After you left, the chief came by. He wanted me to know that the mechanic who looked at the rental found the brakes had been tampered with."

Maryann sat down heavily on a kitchen chair. "Someone deliberately tried to hurt us?"

Jen licked her lips. "Me. They want to hurt me. You're just collateral damage."

"Nice to know." Maryann leaned forward, her elbows on the wooden table. "I don't understand it."

"Neither do I. But the chief's investigating."

"I hope he finds out who's behind this and why."

Jen didn't mention her suspicions regarding her mother. The thought was too painful to endure. Aaron soon returned and they set about baking blueberry corn muffins.

"Don't tell anyone but my secret ingredient is oatmeal. Makes for a much more satisfying and healthy treat."

"Sometimes we bake banana nut muffins," Aaron confided in Maryann. "At Thanksgiving, we baked cranberry pumpkin ones. They were the best. Yummy in the tummy."

"We'll do it again," Jen assured him, hoping no one would kill her between now and then. The thought was so disturbing, that she slammed the muffin tins on the counter with a vengeance.

Maryann gave her a questioning look. "You okay?"

"Of course." She forced a smile. For Aaron's sake she couldn't allow herself to show stress. She wanted her son to have a happy childhood, better than the one she'd had.

Grant Coleman walked into the kitchen. "Ms. Waller, would you come back to the study? I'd like to ask you some questions about what you saw and heard last night."

Maryann raised her eyebrows. "I really can't say much more."

"Not a problem. We should just go over the events. You might remember something more if I ask the right questions."

Maryann shrugged. "Sure, no problem."

As they left the kitchen, Jen thought Grant really seemed to be a first-rate policeman. The thought reassured her.

Chapter Twenty-Two

Mr. Donne welcomed them into his office, polite as ever. "Chief Coleman, Mrs. Stoddard, what can I do for you today?"

They sat down opposite the attorney. Grant Coleman leaned forward placing his muscular forearms on the lawyer's desk, his expression intense.

"I'll get right to the point," Grant said. "Mrs. Stoddard has recently been the object of an anonymous threat. Some unknown party or parties want her to leave town."

The lawyer's watery blue eyes opened wide. "I can't imagine who would do such a thing."

"Neither can Mrs. Stoddard. That's why I've gotten involved."

"What can I do to help?"

"Go over the terms of the will with us if you would."

The attorney turned to Jen. "Mrs. Stoddard, you have a copy of the will. Did you lose it?"

"No, I didn't." She looked to Grant Coleman.

"Mrs. Stoddard showed me the will. But I'm not a lawyer. I need you to explain some things."

"Certainly. What is it you would like to know?"

"Well, sir, first of all, if Mrs. Stoddard should die, who inherits? Does the money and house go to her heirs?"

Mr. Donne sat back in his chair, steepling his fingers. "That's a good question. The estate would only go to Mrs. Stoddard's heirs if she first inherited it. That would mean she lived two years in Mrs. Pritchard's house. Otherwise, the house and the rest of the estate would be divided among sundry charities which Mrs. Pritchard designated."

Grant turned and looked at her. "That's really interesting. So if someone drove Mrs. Stoddard out of the house before two year's time, she wouldn't collect a dime."

"I'm afraid that's correct," the attorney agreed.

Grant was thoughtful for a time. "What about Sara Morrow, Mrs. Pritchard's daughter, how would she benefit if her daughter left town?"

The lawyer appeared perplexed. "I don't see that she would benefit at all."

"Mr. Donne, was Sara Morrow ever in her mother's will?"

"Yes, as a matter of fact, she was. Sara and her mother often argued. After one particularly bitter disagreement, Mrs. Pritchard asked me to change her will to benefit her granddaughter and completely disinherit her daughter. She told me that her granddaughter's husband had just passed away and she was concerned about Mrs. Stoddard's financial security and that of her great grandchild. She wanted them both protected. She said her daughter was a lost cause, a greedy individual who would never change. She wanted her granddaughter to return to her roots." The lawyer turned to Jen. "Your grandmother believed your life and especially that of your child would be better living here than in a city."

Jen was about to say that no one in New York had threatened her or attempted to kill her, dangerous as city life might be perceived. However, she held her tongue.

"I'm sure she meant well," Jen said.

The attorney gave her an approving nod. "Velma was a good woman. She wanted only the best for you and your boy."

"Mr. Donne, can you provide me with a list of the charities that would benefit if Mrs. Stoddard doesn't live in her grandmother's house for the stipulated two year period?"

"I'll have my assistant provide you with that information."

Grant shifted in his seat. "There is one other thing. How is the estate being administered?"

Mr. Donne raised his brows. "Why through my office."

"By you personally?"

"I'm the executor. My nephew Edward is a C.P.A. He is in charge of all our firm's auditing procedures. The funds themselves were originally invested by Mr. Pritchard. His wife took over upon his death. Shortly after Mrs. Pritchard set up the trust for her granddaughter, she had our firm take over the investments. In the last year of her life, she was much too ill to be bothered by such matters."

On leaving Mr. Donne's office, Jen turned to Grant Coleman. "What are you thinking?"

"Something doesn't feel right. Maybe it's just cop instinct. I'll look into the matter. I promise."

Jen felt reassured. She was convinced that Grant was reliable. When he gave his word, he would follow through.

Chapter Twenty-Three

Jen found Maryann and Rob Coleman sharing blueberry muffins and coffee when she returned to the house.

"Where's Aaron?"

Maryann stood up. "Mrs. Higgins phoned. She invited him over to play with her son. So I took him over there. I didn't think you'd mind."

"Not under the circumstances. Thank you."

Rob stood and pulled out a chair for her to sit on. "I just finished putting in the new glass. Window's as good as new."

"As long as no one decides to smash it again."

"Let's hope that's the end of it," Maryann said. "I remember when I was a kid, one of our next door neighbor's sons broke our window practicing baseball."

"Not quite the same thing."

"No, I guess not." Maryann lowered her eyes.

"So Grant's not with you?" Rob brushed the crumbs from his fingers.

"No, but he's promised to continue looking into the matter. I can imagine he has a great deal else on his agenda."

"Yeah, he's a busy guy, but he'll figure this out. He's a good cop. So don't you worry. Tell you what, tonight is The Red Pepper's pizza special. Two for one. Why don't I take us all out? Best pizza anywhere."

Maryann looked to her.

"All right," Jen said. "I know Aaron would love it. Pizza's just about his favorite food. He practically inhales it."

"Great. Six-thirty a good time?"

"Perfect."

By the time Jen had picked up Aaron at the Higgins' house and got him cleaned up, Maryann had already changed into another sundress. It had a stunning floral print bodice that flattered her blond good looks. By comparison, Jen thought she must look quite plain but somehow didn't mind.

"Mom, Mrs. Higgins says there's a swim club and their family are members. We're all going to be invited." Aaron sounded happy and excited.

"Aaron, I don't want to impose on them."

"Mom, you wouldn't be. They really want to have us. Honor bright."

"All right. I'll talk to Mrs. Higgins and we'll see."

Rob picked them up at six-thirty, just as he said he would.

Aaron, in full race horse mode, couldn't be contained. "I'm starving! Let's go." He rushed out the front door heading in the direction of Rob's pick-up truck.

Jen hurried after him. "You're always hungry."

Rob caught up with Aaron. "Okay, let's get going, champ."

Aaron ran ahead again and then waited for them by Rob's pick-up. "Can I go with Rob?"

"Sure," Jen agreed. "We'll meet you there."

"I can squeeze us all in the cab," Rob offered.

Jen shook her head. "You two go ahead. We'll catch up." She watched them drive off before heading toward her car.

"What is it?" Maryann asked. "You looked wistful."

"Just thinking how much Aaron needs a man in his life. We both miss Bill."

Maryann placed her arm around Jen. "I know it can't be easy for either one of you."

"I won't dwell on it. Meantime, we have Rob generously spending time with all of us. He really is a kind man."

"Not like his brother?"

Jen thought of the way Grant had held her in his arms the evening before and kissed her. "The Chief has his moments." She offered a wry smile.

"If you say so. I think he's a little scary. I wouldn't want him for an enemy."

It was all going well until Grant Coleman sauntered into the establishment.

Rob called to his brother. "Hey, Chief, join us. We've got plenty."

Grant looked at them and shook his head. "Sorry. Meeting someone."

Sure enough, he looked around, saw an attractive blonde and slid into the booth opposite her at the rear of the establishment.

"Hot date?" Maryann brows rose in a questioning expression. Jen didn't know why but Maryann's comment bothered her. Kind of silly considering she and Grant had no history together.

"That's no hot date."

"Do tell," Maryann said, leaning forward.

"She's Grant's ex, Cary. I heard she was in town. Hope she's not come to hit him up for money. She's done that in the past. He doesn't owe her anything. She skipped out on him when he was deployed overseas. Dumped him for some sales exec from Minneapolis. I hear she's divorced from another fellow now as well. I got no use for her. Never did like her."

On that she and Rob agreed. Although Jen had to be honest and admit she'd been jealous of Cary who'd been a popular cheerleader back in high school.

"They look attractive together," Jen allowed.

"Think so?" Rob scowled. "He doesn't want anything to do with her. But he's got a good heart. Too good for the likes of her."

"And here I thought your brother was the tough, dangerous type." Maryann teased him obviously hoping to improve Rob's mood.

They watched Grant and his ex. They didn't eat together, Jen observed. Eventually Cary, frowning, rose from the table with an abrupt motion and clicked out of the restaurant on stiletto heels.

"She did not look happy," Maryann whispered to Jen.

"I'm inviting my brother to join us again. He needs company."

"And pizza," Aaron said.

"Got that right, sport."

Rob did most of the talking, but dinner went better than she expected. Every once in a while, Grant looked over at her and Jen wondered what he might be thinking. He remained an enigma for her, a puzzle that she didn't expect to solve any time soon. The man appeared to have many facets, some of them well-hidden. She wished she didn't find him so attractive. She didn't need any more hurt in her life.

Chapter Twenty-Four

Grant phoned ahead setting up an appointment to interview Sara Morrow. He kept his tone casual and she responded by agreeing to see him. No sense showing hostility. It wouldn't help get him any insights or information. He might not like the woman, but no need to make that obvious.

The highway motel she stayed at looked rundown. The rugs and curtains in the seedy lobby showed evidence of wear. Grant asked the bored desk clerk to announce him. After about ten minutes Sara Morrow joined him in the lobby. He assumed her purpose in keeping him waiting was deliberate since he'd called ahead. She was making a point.

Her hair sported a bad dye job, unreal red color, teased and sprayed giving her a phony look. He noted the contrast to her daughter. Jennifer Stoddard's silky hair framed her face in soft waves of rich, dark amber.

Sara Morrow's face had formed deep wrinkles around the mouth as if she frowned a good deal. She'd dressed in pink slacks and a print blouse which had a noticeable stain in front.

"Ms. Morrow. Thank you for seeing me."

She pointed a long, blood red fingernail at him. "I don't know what this is about but I haven't broken any laws."

Grant kept his face devoid of expression. "No one's accusing you of anything. But you should know that your daughter has been the object of certain threats."

"What kind of threats?" Her eyes narrowed.

"Why don't we discuss this in a more private place?"

"No thanks. As you can see, the lobby is empty. We can talk right here. Besides, I really have nothing to say."

"Fine."

They sat opposite each other on dated green Danish modern chairs.

"You think I had something to do with threatening Jennifer?"

"I don't know. Did you?"

"I don't know anything about that."

"What about your friend? Frank is it? Weren't you both expecting your daughter to give you some money?"

Sara Morrow stood up, folding her arms over her ample chest. "I don't like what you're implying. Of course, I expected my daughter to share the inheritance my mother left her with me. It was my mother after all. I can only assume she wasn't in her right mind at the time she had that crooked lawyer draw up a new will leaving everything to Jennifer. The whole thing is crazy. Frank thinks I should challenge the will. I think he's right. Sure I got irritated when Jen refused to share with me. Wouldn't anybody?"

"Ms. Morrow, you should know that your daughter hasn't inherited anything as yet. She won't unless she lives in the Pritchard house for two years. Were you aware of that fact?"

"I need money now," she said, "not in the future."

Grant stood to his full six foot three inch height, towering over Sara Morrow. He was aware that she hadn't actually answered his question.

"Planning to stay in town?"

"Absolutely."

"Why? Are you planning on harassing your daughter?"

"Why I'm here has nothing to do with you. I've done nothing illegal." She placed her hands on her hips.

"Best to keep a distance from your daughter." With that, he turned and left the motel lobby.

Maryann frowned at her laptop. Nothing new in her e-mails. There were certain times of the year when job hunting was hardly worth the bother. August seemed to be one of them. Executives were on vacation. Things had slowed down at a lot of companies. Workers chose to do the bare minimum. It would pick up in September. She'd find a new position when she returned to the city. She wouldn't confine her search to Big Pharma either. She'd contacted headhunters who seemed positive they could help. No guarantees but she preferred to maintain a positive outlook.

"Anything?" Jen stood out in the hallway outside her bedroom door.

"No, not yet."

Jen provided a reassuring smile. "I wish you didn't have to go back to New York at all. I'd like it if you could stay right here with us. Aaron loves you and so do I."

Maryann stood up and hugged her friend. "It's nice to be appreciated. I wish I could afford to stay longer but it isn't possible."

"I'm going up to the attic. I remember going up there as a child. There are lots of interesting things lying about. Want to join me?"

"All right. Where's Aaron?"

Jen made a face. "Would you believe he's gone swimming with the Higgins family? They belong to a club and offered to include him. Aaron was delighted."

"I'll bet."

As Maryann followed her friend up the steep, creaky staircase that led to the old mansion's attic, she felt a sense of unease. The place certainly had atmosphere. Maybe a little too much. She shivered.

"There's a lot of wonderful stuff in the attic. I used to love to play dress up here as a kid. There are chests full of amazing old clothes. As I recall there are some Tiffany lamps and Wedgwood vases. I'd love to sell off some of it to an antique dealer. But they're not mine as yet."

"They will be yours eventually," Maryann said.

Jen moved her head from side to side. "Two years is a long time. We'll see."

Maryann stepped fully into the attic and blinked, adjusting her eyes to the darkened room. She was greeted by dust and decay. She pushed away some cobwebs as she sought the treasures Jen expected to find.

She was drawn to a trunk in the corner. The workmanship, exquisite and ornate, had endured. Quite an exotic piece. "I'd like a look at this."

"Feel free to explore," Jen said.

Maryann opened the chest. It smelled of mothballs, not the most pleasant odor in the world. But she was rewarded with several lovely hand-made quilts, one a patchwork, the other a floral design.

"These are a delight."

Jen looked over at the quilts Maryann held up. "They've been in the family forever and are very well-preserved."

"I'm really into folk art," Maryann said.

"Then you've come to the right place. Lots of history here. Family secrets as well."

"Do tell." Maryann raised an eyebrow with interest. "Anything you care to share?"

"My grandmother knew it all, not me."

"Did she keep a diary?"

"I think she did as a matter of fact, but I have no idea where it is. I've stayed out of her old room, maybe as a sign of respect."

"My parents enjoyed antiquing. When I was little I'd go along with them. I learned a lot about antiques from them."

Jen looked up from the delicate china cups she was examining. "I didn't know that."

"Most interesting by far is the length that crooks will go to put one over on unsuspecting buyers. It's like art forgery fakes. They use a lot of high tech these days to perpetrate frauds."

Jen tossed back her head of wavy auburn hair. "That's why provenance is so important."

Maryann put down the quilts lost in thought. "You can't always get the provenance at auctions or estate sales."

"You're right."

Maryann looked deeper into the trunk. There were women's clothes all neatly packed away. Most of them had yellowed with age, but they were period clothing of fine quality. At the bottom, wrapped snugly in fine linen was a beautiful gown. It looked like a ball gown of some sort and strangely it appeared as if it were new, as if it had never aged at all. She was intrigued by it. She brought it out and held it up by the window to see it better. The style was Victorian, a silk and satin confection with seed pearls generously sewn into the bodice. It appeared to be pure white. With it was a gossamer snowy veil. So this was someone's wedding dress. The workmanship was incredible. She'd never seen anything more beautiful in her life. The gown shimmered with an unearthly glow as ethereal as a moonbeam. When she shook it out, something fell to the floor. It too was carefully wrapped so as to preserve it. With careful hands, she gently rolled back the linen binding the object.

A doll! But not an ordinary doll. No, this doll was vivid and alive in looks. It too appeared Victorian in design. Golden hair and bright blue eyes that glowed with ethereal light. Just amazing! Even more remarkable, the doll was dressed in a wedding gown which seemed to be a perfect replica of the one she'd been examining. Someone had a remarkable talent with needle and thread.

"Wow, did you ever see this before?"

Jen give a quick nod. "I have. I even asked my grandmother about it. She told me to leave it alone. Apparently, it has a sad history. The girl who would have worn that wedding gown died shortly before the ceremony was to take place. There had been an influenza epidemic and she was one of the victims. In grief, her parents put the gown away. I guess the doll must have been an effigy of her. Probably those quilts were made for her wedding as well."

Maryann shivered, although the day was a warm one. She placed the gown and quilts back in their chest.

Jen sneezed. The sound seemed loud. "I'll have to get Linda and her crew up here to clean. There's too much dust for us to continue our exploration. Let's have lunch. I could do with something cold to drink."

Downstairs the doorbell rang and then someone banged at the front door. She and Jen exchanged surprised looks.

"Expecting anyone?"

Jen shook her head. "Guess we better find out who's come to call."

Chapter Twenty-Five

"Hello, Mother, is this a friendly visit?"

Sara's face had flushed an unbecoming shade of red. Jen assumed from her mother's manner that Sara's appearance reflected her bad mood as much as the heat of the day.

Frank followed her mother into the foyer. She hadn't invited either of them into the house, but they appeared to think it their right to enter. Maryann came up behind Jen.

"Jennifer, why did you send that police person to see me?"

"I didn't."

"No? Well, that's not the impression I got. He said something about you being threatened. You know I did no such thing. Why would I? Anyway I'm willing to leave town if that's what you really want but I expect you're going to write me a check. Aren't you?"

"I don't have much money to spare right now. Not until the estate becomes mine. That won't be for two years, Mother. I think you already know that."

"Frank and I are staying in the area. We've decided to hire a lawyer of our own. My mother wasn't herself when she changed her will in favor of you. For all I know, you used undue influence on an old woman suffering from dementia. Anyway, I'm challenging the will. I have just as much right to the money as you do, in fact more. I should warn you. It could get ugly. I'll see you in court." Her mother signaled her boyfriend to follow.

Maryann shut the door. "No offense, Jen, but that woman's nothing like you. Are you sure you weren't adopted?"

She offered a small smile. "I'm afraid not."

"Greedy is how I'd describe her." Maryann scrunched her nose as if she'd smelled some foul odor.

"My grandmother once said she felt Grandfather spoiled my mother as a child. He'd give her everything she wanted. Grandmother had to be the bad guy, the disciplinarian. They'd had another child, a boy, who died in early childhood. I don't know all the facts. Anyway when my mother was born, Grandfather felt jubilant. And then it turned out that Grandmother couldn't have any more children. So Grandfather treated Mother like a princess."

"But your grandmother didn't?"

Jen gazed off, transported to another time. "No, Grandmother's ethics were ingrained. She had high moral standards. Grandfather acted as something of a buffer between the two of them. When Mom's marriage to my father fell apart, she blamed my grandparents for encouraging the marriage in the first place."

"She didn't love your father?"

"Maryann, I don't think my mother is capable of loving anyone... maybe not even herself. She and I never really connected on any meaningful level. There were maids and nannies. We spent very little time together when I was growing up."

"I didn't realize that." Maryann's expression conveyed sympathy.

"Hey, I'm an adult now. I just hope not to make those kinds of mistakes with Aaron. That's why I didn't go back to work after he was born. I wanted to spend as much time as possible with my child when he was little."

"My mother went back to teaching as soon as she could. Not that I blame her. It's tough staying home taking care of little kids."

"True, but I think it's the most important job there is even if it doesn't involve a pay check." Jen realized her opinion on the matter probably seemed old-fashioned. "Of course, with Aaron in school, I really do want to return to work—although it doesn't appear there are many positions open to bio-chemists around here."

"No, it doesn't," Maryann agreed. "You and I are going to have to get creative."

The doorbell rang again. They exchanged looks.

"You think she's back?" Maryann's green eyes opened wider.

"I hope not." With some trepidation, Jen opened the front door for the second time today.

Rob Coleman stood there. Jen let out the breath she been holding.

"We finished the job we were doing earlier than I expected today. Thought I'd drop by and check on those cracks I've been meaning to fix in your cellar."

"Have you had lunch yet?" Jen asked.

"No, I'll stop off at the diner later."

"Why don't you join us? Maryann and I were just about to throw together some sandwiches."

"Sounds good, but I don't want to intrude."

"You won't be."

They walked out to the kitchen at a leisurely pace. Jen smiled to herself noting the way Rob looked at Maryann. There could be no mistaking what that look meant.

They fixed grilled cheese and tomato sandwiches garnished with green olives, then chatted over iced tea. Rob ate three sandwiches to their one.

"Hope I'm not being a hog." He wiped his mouth appreciatively with a paper napkin.

"You work hard. You need to eat more." Maryann stood up and took the plates, placing them in the sink.

"You make good sandwiches." Rob patted his hard stomach. "So where's the little guy today?"

"Swimming with the Higgins family. I'll reciprocate and host their son tomorrow." Jen topped off everyone's beverages. She had a thought and turned back to Rob. "Maybe I can fix a picnic lunch. Rob, you must know some appropriate places to take the children."

"Sure do." Rob proceeded to provide helpful suggestions.

Jen thought to herself that he also provided good company. She hoped Maryann felt the same.

Rob went down to cellar after lunch and looked around. There were some cracks in the foundation that still needed work. He'd see to that. No problem. But as he examined the area, Rob saw something that disturbed him. One of the window panes appeared to be broken. That hadn't been the case before. It hadn't been caused by an animal. He felt certain of that.

Someone had tried to pry open the window. It could have been a vandal but he doubted it. The window was too small to allow anyone to enter, even a child. Viewing it with a close eye, he saw some dried blood. Not a practiced burglar he thought but someone prowling around outside the house. Could it be the same person that had thrown the rock with the threatening message through the upstairs window? He'd talk to his brother about it. The women would have to be informed as well. He didn't like the idea of making them feel more nervous or insecure. But they did need to be aware.

Chapter Twenty-Six

Grant had a busy day at police headquarters. He'd even eaten lunch at his desk. Bloomingvale tended to be a quiet, peaceful town, but there had been a robbery at the gas station. With a small police force, they were kept on their toes. His brother's phone call proved disturbing.

"What bothered me about that broken window was why anyone would bother with it." Rob had a point.

Grant drummed his fingers on the top of his wooden desk. "Clearly, this person wasn't trying to get into the house through that small window. I can only think of one reason."

"Which is?"

"To place something in the cellar meant to further persuade and convince Jennifer Stoddard to leave the house."

"Like a grenade?"

"Rob, it doesn't have to be anything that destructive. Could be this person intended to set off a smoke bomb or something similar as another warning, an attempt to further intimidate Mrs. Stoddard."

"Who do you think is responsible?"

"Right now, I've got no idea who's behind this. Generally, I'd say the motive for harassing Jennifer Stoddard and getting her to move out of the house would be financial gain. But I don't see who's going to benefit. I'll check out those charities though. I've already spoken to Sara Morrow. Let me see if I can get more info on that boyfriend of hers as well. You going over to Mom's for dinner tonight?"

"I'll be there," Rob said.

"Good. We can discuss this more then."

Grant hung up the phone and continued to drum his fingers on his desk. Something was going on that he didn't understand. He needed to collect more information. He went out front to the main office and found Burt Russell at work on a report.

"Could you come into my office for a few minutes?"

"Sure, Chief." Burt, a raw-boned farm boy, had joined the force two years ago.

"I want you to shadow some people for me." He gave Burt the particulars. "At this point, I want to know who this Frank character is. So follow at a distance. Take an unmarked car not a cruiser. Watch for them to drive over the speed limit, run a red light, anything at all you can pull them over for. I want you to get Frank's information and run him through the system. And I need that information as soon as possible."

"Got it, Chief. I'll nail him for you."

His next move was to phone James Donne's office and get a copy of the charities Mrs. Pritchard named in her will. He needed to find out if they were legit.

He got busy again himself with leads on the gas station robbery. Apparently, it was a familiar M.O. in the area. Three such robberies had occurred in a hundred-mile radius. He made a few calls to other law enforcement officers and got more details.

It was five p.m. before he managed to get over to the law office. After a cursory examination of the list, Grant decided to discuss the information with Jennifer Stoddard and get her take on it. He didn't expect that she could be particularly helpful, but like his mother's chicken soup when he had a cold, it wouldn't hurt either.

The doorbell rang at five-thirty p.m., and Jen went to answer it. She was taken back by seeing Grant Coleman standing there. She stared at him for a moment before inviting him into the house. Whenever she saw him, she noticed that her heart beat faster.

She led him into the living room. "Can I offer you something to drink?"

"No thanks. I want to talk to you about something."

"Have a seat."

He surprised her by sitting down on the comfortable sofa and indicating the spot beside him. Reluctantly, she sat but kept her posture stiffly erect. Strange how the room began to shrink, to practically close in on her.

"I'm looking into what's been happening to you. I brought by that list of charities Donne mentioned. Will you take a look with me and see if you know anything about them?" He showed her a photocopied list which she viewed with concentration.

"Some of these charities are well-known and of course I've heard of them. Some I don't know anything about. The Forrest Foundation? Mr. Forrest came to the house when I first arrived. He let me know that my grandmother was very generous to his charity. He practically demanded that I continue to make donations of a similar kind. When I told him that I was unable at present to make that kind of financial commitment, he became huffy."

His gray eyes searched her face. "He tried to strong arm you? You think he might be behind your recent problems?"

Jen shook her head. "I'd hate to believe that. I mean his charity did sound worthy. And I told him when the estate was settled I'd certainly make a contribution."

"Did that seem to placate him?"

She nibbled her lower lip. "Not really."

"Okay, then he's a person of interest, someone I need to have a conversation with. Anyone else?"

She studied the list. "I didn't know Dr. Kramer ran a free clinic."

"He does. There are lots of poor people who don't have proper health insurance coverage. Dr. Gus and Ella provide free medical one day a week. Looks like your grandmother made generous donations to keep the clinic going. They are named as beneficiaries if you don't fulfill the terms of the will."

"Dr. Kramer was my grandmother's doctor. He told me she died in her sleep, probably of a heart attack."

Grant raised his eyebrows. "Did he do an autopsy?"

"Not as far as I know. I suppose there was no reason for it. My grandmother was old and ill. Still, he did say that she had been improving."

"Anyone else you recognize on this list?"

Another name surprised her. "Eric Higgins would also benefit it seems. My grandmother provided for his animal shelter. But the Higgins are such kind, friendly people. My son Aaron loves playing with their son, Bobby." Jen shook her head. "No, neither he nor Dr. Kramer would be harassing me. It's just not possible."

"I hope you're right," Grant said, "but people get funny when there's a lot of money involved. Even when there's not so much."

"I feel badly about taking up your time. Maybe these are just pranks of some sort. I'm certain you have more important matters that need your attention."

"I want to make sure everything goes all right for you." His gaze probed and searched.

Jen felt sudden unease. What might he be thinking? What suspicions lurked in his cynical mind? "What you really mean is you don't trust me. You don't believe someone is behind this, someone who wishes me ill." She was finding it hard to hold on to her temper.

"Don't tell me what I mean." His expression became severe as he gritted his teeth. They were practically nose to nose, and his nostrils were flaring like a bull seeing a red cape.

Good, let him get angry too; she didn't really care.

"I'm not the kind of person who sneaks around. I'm looking out for everybody's welfare. That's an important part of my job. Can't you understand that? Don't misinterpret my questions. I do believe what you've told me. Didn't I say that before?"

His hand brushed her arm as if to bring her to face him directly. Where he touched, she felt as if licked by a flame. An alarm sounded in her brain.

"Sorry," he said, seeing her shrink from his touch.

She didn't speak; she couldn't.

"I'm not trying to intimidate or harass you. I want to help you in any way I can. Will you please believe that? I know we haven't gotten off to a good start. Maybe that's partly my fault. But I do think I could help you if you'll let me."

She recognized that he was being conciliatory and sincere. Probably she should meet him half-way. Sometimes, she conceded, she could be over sensitive. "I promise if I need help, I'll ask for it."

"Will you?"

She felt her cheeks heat with color. "What's that supposed to mean?"

He turned and gave her a sharp look, his face all hard angles and planes.

"Rob phoned me earlier."

She let out the breath she'd been holding. "He shouldn't have bothered you. One of your patrol officers could have come by."

"If it was just a matter of someone trying to pry open a cellar window. But it seems to be part of a pattern. That's why I'm involving myself in the situation. I'd like to see that window if you don't mind."

They went downstairs together and he examined the window in question. He made some notes and used a kit to dust for prints, all of which made Jen feel more uneasy than ever.

"Here's what I'd like to do. I think we should set up surveillance cameras around the perimeter of your house as soon as possible."

"Is that really necessary?" She put her hand on his and then quickly removed it as if she'd been zapped. It made her uncomfortable to touch him and yet at the same time, she'd liked it too much. "I'll have to think about it."

He squared his jaw. Funny, she hadn't noticed that small sexy cleft in his chin before.

"I don't see that there's anything to think about. I'll take care of it. We'll place the equipment discreetly so no one knows it's there."

She let out a deep sigh. "All right. Whatever you think best."

They walked back toward the stairs side by side. She felt hot and dizzy yet chilled at the same time. He took her arm as if to assist her but that only made her feel all the more unsteady. If she didn't act more in control, he was sure to be convinced she was a wimp.

He looked at her and his eyes seemed to settle on the curve of her lips. For a moment, she had the strangest feeling that he wanted to kiss her. Stranger still was the awareness that she really wanted him to do it. She felt an overwhelming desire to be held and caressed by him.

He pulled her into his arms. His lips found hers. Their mouth joined in a deep kiss, hungry with need. Her pulse began to pound. It took every ounce of her willpower and self-control to pull away from that powerful magnetic attraction. What was she thinking? This was strictly a professional relationship. He didn't even really like her. And she had no business thinking of him as anything other than the chief of police. She wasn't a high school senior with a teenage crush anymore but an adult, grown woman. She better start acting like one.

Chapter Twenty-Seven

Grant lumbered into the kitchen, further filling the small room. He kissed their mother on the cheek and affectionately messed the top of his sisters' heads both of whom let out squeals of complaints.

"You nearly missed dinner." Rob moved over making room for his brother. "I intended to eat your portion."

"No way," Grant said.

"So did you take a look at that broken cellar window at the Pritchard house?"

"I did." Grant frowned.

"And what's the verdict?"

"I'm going to put in camera surveillance."

Mom filled a plate for Grant. "Is someone causing trouble for that nice woman?"

"I'm not certain what's going on." Grant ran his fingers through his hair in a distracted manner.

"But you'll find out?" Her question seemed more like a command.

"Yeah, I'll find out."

"You see Maryann while you were at the house?"

Grant eyeballed him. "No, she wasn't around."

"Mrs. Stoddard say where she was?"

Grant folded his arms over his chest. "No, she didn't. Why are you so interested?"

Rob didn't like his brother's tone of voice. "I happen to like her. You got a problem with that?" He narrowed his eyes.

"Just be careful, okay? City women look down on people like us."

Mom dumped the filled plate in front of Grant. "I think you're being unfair. Both of those young women are polite and courteous, easy to work with."

"Don't you mean work for." Grant gave his mother a hard look and she stared back at him. They appeared poised for a confrontation.

"Hey, let's not get hostile here." Rob, a peacemaker by nature, did his best to diffuse what could be a volatile discussion. Grant and his mother had similar personalities. Both had tempers. Rob changed the subject, telling a joke one of his crew had shared earlier in the day. The tension in the kitchen relaxed.

Grant had just gotten to his desk when Burt Russell burst in. "Chief, I got the information you wanted, you know on that guy. Franklin Kraulley."

"Sara Morrow's pal?"

"That's the one." Burt looked pleased with himself.

"So spill."

Burt sat down on the chair opposite Grant's desk and leaned forward on his elbows. "I tailed them all day yesterday. You figured right. He ran a stop sign. I pulled them over and got his I.D., ran it through the system. Guy's from Chicago. He's got priors. Mostly petty stuff but not what you'd call an upstanding citizen."

"Anything related to burglary or auto theft?"

"Both."

Grant raised his dark eyebrows. "Gets more interesting. Any violent crimes?"

"None that I could find. Strictly theft and nothing big. He served some time. Is he the person of interest you're looking for?"

Grant shifted in his chair. "Honestly, I don't know. But this is helpful info. Could be that Jennifer Stoddard's mother and boyfriend Frank are doing a number on her, trying to get her to leave the Pritchard house. I think Sara Morrow believes if she gets rid of her daughter, her claim to her mother's estate will be strengthened."

Burt stared at him. "Chief, how do you mean get rid of?"

"I'm not really sure. Could just be mischief to frighten her into leaving town."

"You don't think they'd try to kill her, do you?"

Grant shook his head. "When you can, keep an eye on those two. I'm going to see what else I can find out. My impression has been that Ms. Morrow plans to get her hands on her mother's estate by legal means. But you never know about people. Sometimes they just snap." He brought his thumb and forefinger together for emphasis. "That's when we have to come into it and clean things up. The Morrow woman's got a mean streak. Doesn't sound like the boyfriend's any better. When there's money involved as a motive, it brings out the ugliness in some people."

Burt nodded, his expression solemn.

Chapter Twenty-Eight

Jen and Maryann took Aaron, Bobby Higgins and his sister Pam on a picnic the following day. They did some hiking, bird watching and settled by a local pond to eat their lunch of turkey sandwiches, potato salad, lemonade and apples. The respite felt pleasant and idyllic.

"We ride our bikes out here a lot," Bobby told them.

Jen realized she'd have to purchase a bike for Aaron if they remained in Bloomingvale. It seemed both Bobby and Pam were competent riders. Pam, the older and more mature of the Higgins children, provided good companionship for Maryann and herself. She didn't seem to mind the company of adults. Maggie Higgins had trained her daughter to be polite and helpful. Pam collected used paper plates, cups and plastic utensils to throw away in a nearby trash can.

"Do you want to be an animal doctor like your father?" Jen asked Pam.

"Bobby and I both want that. Our dad loves animals and so do we. Bobby and I help out at the animal shelter as often as we can. It means a lot to all of us."

The boys tossed leftover bread to the ducks in the pond. Then they picked up rocks to throw and create ripples in the pond. But their attention span had limitations. Soon they roamed about with restless energy.

Jen decided to drive everyone back to town and browse around the local stores for a while.

"Let's go to the bookstore first and see if we can find some interesting reading material."

Pam exclaimed her pleasure but Bobby groaned.

"We have to read all year in school. I'd like to practice shooting hoops or hitting baseballs."

Jen realized not being an athlete herself created a definite disadvantage in dealing with boys like Bobby Higgins. Her own son would soon want to go out for sports teams like his friend. "We have a soccer ball back at the house. Why don't we find it and you can practice with that?"

She felt relieved when Bobby expressed an interest in soccer. Jen realized this activity was one her husband would have shared with his son if he had lived. Aaron hadn't said anything but she knew he felt his father's loss as acutely as she did.

On the following day, Bobby and Pam had dental appointments. Jen and Maryann decided to take Aaron for a walk on Main Street. Just to make certain it was a fun trip for Aaron, Jen visited Bigelow's Bakery first. They picked out treats and a fresh baked loaf of bread for lunch.

Mrs. Bigelow made a fuss over Aaron. "Young man, I think you're going to be one of my best customers." She winked at him and handed him a chocolate chip cookie. "This one's on the house."

"I can't let you do that," Jen said.

"No, really I want him to have it."

The baker came from the back, his face rosy, hair pure white. His rounded midsection gave testimony to the fact that he enjoyed his own culinary efforts.

"Aggie, I see you're giving away our profits again."

"Nonsense. This handsome young man loves our baked goods. He deserves something special."

"Hello, Mr. Bigelow," Jen said. "We're new in town."

"Mrs. Pritchard's granddaughter. You remember Mrs. Pritchard, don't you, Wendell?"

"Of course. An excellent customer. Young ladies, you know anyone who wants to buy a bakery?" He looked from Jen to Maryann. "I'm ready to retire to Florida, but my wife refuses to close the bakery. She'll only go if someone trustworthy is running the place."

"I'm afraid we're not bakers. But I wish I were."

"I'd share my recipes with the right person."

"If I meet any bakers, I'll let you know."

"You do that." He shook Jen's hand with a vigorous motion.

They took their purchases and left the bakery. Next door a vacant store looked forlorn. Maryann studied it. "If I were an entrepreneur, I would buy the bakery, knock down the wall between it and the other store, then turn that area into a coffee shop. People could buy bakery goodies, then sit down and have them with a latte or espresso or cappuccino."

"I don't know," Jen said. "People around here go to the diner for coffee."

"That's true. But I'd do a more upscale version."

"The town is surrounded by farms."

Maryann bit her lower lip lost in thought. "That's where advertising and promotion comes in. The internet is one way to go with that. And look, the bookstore is on the other side of the empty store. Just saying the location has potential. I worked in retail establishments summers during high school and college. I have some savvy."

Jen shrugged. "I know nothing whatever about business. I won't argue with you about a hypothetical business."

"Right. There's no point. It's just interesting to consider. I suppose I always do wonder if I could make a go of a business. But investment capital is a big drawback. And most businesses do fail. Still I believe I could make one work."

They visited the bookstore next. Aaron loved to read just as she did. So it was no problem at all getting him to choose several books. Jen and Maryann each treated themselves to books as well. Maryann's choice was a nonfiction book on marketing that struck Jen as dull as dust. She herself chose a mystery novel that featured an archaeologist on a dig.

"Wow, you people are good customers," the pretty young woman behind the cash register said. "Can I help you look for anything else?"

"Not right now," Jen said. "We just wanted some summer reading."

"I'm Terrie Prentice. My mom owns this shop. We don't get much business these days. Mom says we're barely breaking even what with the library just up the street and people buying bargain e-books on the internet."

"I'm sorry to hear that," Jen said. "Bookstores are my favorite places, but I do confess to liking libraries too. I'm not much of an internet person though."

"Mom, can I get this?" Aaron was holding a beautifully illustrated bookmark with all sorts of sailing ships on it.

"Good idea. Terrie, please include it in our order."

After they left the bookstore, Jen turned to Maryann. "What about the bookstore serving coffee? Do you think that would help their business?"

Maryann blinked thoughtfully. "I doubt it. It's not helping the brick and mortar bookstores in the malls all that much. People take books and magazines, sit down with the coffee they order and slobber all over the reading materials. It's been my observation that they don't buy much of what they read. Sure the bookstores make some money on the coffee and food they sell, but it's not a good deal for publishers. The small publishers don't even bother with bookstores anymore."

"You're a downer," Jen said.

"Hey, just telling it like it is. Got to build a better mousetrap to succeed."

"Wish I knew what I wanted to do when I grow up," Jen said.

Aaron turned to her. "Mommy, aren't you grown up already?"

Maryann laughed. "He's got you there."

"Sweetie, what I meant is that I'm not sure what direction my life is going to take. When you go to school, I'd like to go back to work. I'm just not certain what I should be doing."

Aaron's looked up at her with solemn dark brown eyes much like her own. "You'll find something good to do. You're real smart."

Jen smiled as she placed her arm around her son. "Thank you for your vote of confidence. I know what you're going to do when you grow up. You're going into the diplomatic corps because you always know just the right thing to say."

Chapter Twenty-Nine

Grant and Burt Russell arrived at the Pritchard house at 9 a.m.. He planned to install surveillance cameras. As they passed Jen Stoddard's white car in the driveway, he became aware the vehicle didn't look right. As they came closer, he observed that the tires were flat. Had someone let the air out? A kid prank?

"Burt, stop here. Let's look at this."

They got down and examined the tires. There were slash marks. Grant shook his head. This kept getting worse. He pulled out his cell phone. Dave Stuart answered on the third ring. Grant explained the situation. "Can you come out here or send somebody?" Dave indicated he could.

Grant turned to Burt. "We better give the lady the bad news."

Jennifer Stoddard answered the door dressed in denim shorts and a peach silky short-sleeved shirt. Her wavy auburn hair had been pulled back. She wore no make-up, but in his opinion didn't need any.

"Chief, this is a surprise," she said.

"We came to install the cameras."

"Please come in. Is it really necessary?"

"Oh, it's very necessary." Grant exchanged a look with Burt.

"I'll just start finding the right locations for these." Burt looked uncomfortable.

"You do that," Grant said. "Front and rear. Sides as well."

Burt left the house as fast as possible.

"He's certainly in a hurry. The thing is, I feel foolish taking up so much of your time and trouble." Her tone of voice seemed earnest and direct.

He noticed the dark brown of her irises. She had large, expressive eyes, a small, pert nose and full, generous lips. Why would he observe those things? He felt annoyed with himself.

"My job is to serve and protect." The words came out sounding gruff.

She blinked at him. "Sorry. I didn't mean to offend you. But I didn't expect you'd do the work yourself."

"I'm pretty handy." The truth was, he wanted to see her again, but he wasn't going to admit that. He cleared his throat. "There's something you should know. Whoever's been harassing you is at it again. All four of your tires have been slashed."

She walked into the parlor and sat down heavily on one of the chairs. "Oh, no. I can't believe this. I just don't understand why anyone would hate me so much."

He expected her to cry at any moment, but she didn't. She straightened her spine and got to her feet again. "I'll do whatever it takes to find out who's behind this."

He hadn't expected her to show so much courage. He admitted to a grudging respect.

"We're going to find out who's been doing this," he promised. "And we're going to put an end to it."

Without meaning to do it, he touched her hand with his own much larger one. For his gesture of compassion, he received an unexpected jolt. It startled him. There seemed to be real chemistry between them. She looked up at him with a look that almost appeared to be adoration. It jarred him. He must be imagining things. He needed to get more sleep, maybe drink another cup of coffee. All of a sudden he felt about her the way he'd felt back in high school when they'd sat beside each other in English class and worked on that project together—before everything changed.

"Dave Stuart will be by later. He'll talk to you about the tires. Meantime, you'll want to let your insurance company know what happened."

"My rates will increase. I think I'm better off just paying out of pocket. Besides there's a large deductible."

He gave a curt nod. "Up to you."

"I better look at the car." She followed him outside. "I still don't understand any of this."

They were soon joined by Jennifer Stoddard's friend, the one his brother seemed so taken with, as well as her son. The little boy looked up at him with some trepidation.

"Are you a real policeman?"

"Yes, son, I am."

"I overheard my mom and Maryann talking. Were you mean to my mom?"

"Aaron!" He watched Jennifer Stoddard's face and neck color and felt amused.

"I'll do my best to be polite to your mother from now on. How's that?"

"Okay, I guess." Grant noticed the boy had small freckles that spread like ants over his nose. He was fairer than his mother but looked a lot like her.

"Maryann, could you fix Aaron's breakfast?"

"Sure thing." Maryann held out her hand and Aaron took it.

When Maryann and Aaron were back inside the house, Jennifer Stoddard turned to him. "I apologize. I believe he heard me complain about you writing me that ticket."

"Yeah, nothing like kids to tell it like it is."

"I'm not angry at you anymore." Her cheeks flushed.

"Good to know."

"I realize you were just doing your job."

And then some, if he were honest. But he said nothing. The tension between them intensified.

"I guess I better leave you to your work. Thank you for helping us."

With that, she hurried into the house. His eyes thoughtfully trailed after her.

Chapter Thirty

Maryann had been working at her laptop for several hours when she became aware of loud sounds coming from somewhere downstairs. Alarmed, she called to Jen but got no answer. Then she remembered Jen mentioned something about going marketing and taking Aaron with her. Maryann had been too absorbed in her job searches at the time to pay much attention.

She heard the noises again. Who or what was making them? She'd been barefoot but now put on her bedroom slippers and hurried down the hall and the stairs. She could now discern that the sounds were coming from the basement. With some caution and trepidation, Maryann took the creaking stairs down.

"Who's there?"

"Just me." Rob's voice floated up to her.

She breathed a sigh of relief. "You scared me."

"Sorry about that. I had some more work to do down here."

She nearly tripped on the last step. Strong arms reached up to catch her.

"Careful there. Those slippers are mighty flimsy. No traction on them either."

"Thank you. You can let go of me now." But he didn't. Rob continued to hold her close.

"Why don't I walk you back upstairs?"

"Really, I'm fine." She pulled away from him, not feeling fine at all. Being close to Rob disturbed her.

"I could use a cold drink about now. What about you?"

"We have fruit juice, iced tea."

"Just water. Join me?"

They went to the kitchen where the late morning sun beautified the room. A nice breeze blew through the sky blue curtains. Rob helped her set up several glasses of water with ice. Then they sat down together at the hardwood table and chairs.

"I suppose I needed a break as well." She took a few sips. The water cooled her inner thermostat.

Rob held the glass against his forehead. "Feels good. Gotta keep hydrated in this hot weather. So what have you been doing?"

"Same old. I've been checking postings for job opportunities that are appropriate for me."

"And I suppose these job opportunities are all in New York City?" His tone had a casual ring but his eyes searched hers like torches.

She looked away. "Of course, that's where I'm looking. There are several good possibilities. I just have to push for interviews."

He took her hand and held it in his firm grasp. "From what you've told me, these companies treat employees rotten. There's no loyalty. They use you, chew you up, then spit you out when it suits them."

"The corporate world is ruthless, but the companies do pay well."

Rob shook his head. "There ought to be a better way to operate."

"Everybody looks to their bottom line. It's nothing personal. Just business."

Rob shrugged. "It's personal when you're the one getting fired."

Maryann withdrew her hand from his. "It's called downsizing or reorganizing."

"I know a euphemism when I hear one."

She raised an eyebrow.

He gave her a knowing look. "You didn't think I knew what a word like euphemism meant, did you?"

"We hardly know each other." She squirmed in her chair.

"Maryann, I'm not educated the way you are. I attended vo-tech in high school and then got just two years of community college at night after leaving the service, but I'm not ignorant."

"I never meant to imply that."

He smiled at her, a warm, vibrant smile that heated her blood all over again.

"You haven't told me how you hurt your leg."

"Don't think I will. I don't dwell on negative things."

"You said your brother also served. Was he injured too?"

"Not physically. Let's just say that like me, he decided a lifetime military career wasn't what he wanted after all." Rob took a long swallow of water. She saw the strong muscles in his throat move.

"Do you live with your family?"

"No, I rent a small place. I bought some land a ways out of town and I'm working on building my own house."

She smiled. "That must be a good feeling."

"It is." He took another gulp of water and then sucked on an ice cube. "Someday I'd like to have a real home, a wife and children. Maybe a few pets."

"Sounds nice."

"Just need to find the right woman." He threw her a meaningful look.

She stared down at her hands holding the glass and then traced a pattern in the condensation. She didn't know how to respond.

Jen spared her by arriving back at the house. She and Aaron walked into the kitchen each carrying packages.

"I thought I heard voices out here."

"Are there more packages?" Rob got to his feet and took the grocery bags Jen and Aaron held.

"Several more in the trunk of the car."

"Be right back with them." Rob left with Aaron trailing behind him.

"I'll help too." He smiled at the boy's eagerness.

"So you and Rob looked pretty cozy just now. I'm sorry if I interrupted anything." Jen gave her a knowing look.

Maryann felt herself blush. "It wasn't like that. Okay, maybe it was," she conceded.

"It's plain to see that Rob is enamored of you."

"Let's not talk about this right now. He'll be back in a few moments."

Jen viewed her with an intent look. "Sure, another time."

Maryann didn't respond, just offering a quick nod. She made her escape hurrying back upstairs to the safety of her computer screen. She didn't like the confused way Rob caused her to feel. She avoided strong emotions. Time to find herself another job, and soon.

Chapter Thirty-One

Jen brought Aaron over to the Higgins' house in the afternoon. She'd purchased cookies from the bakery that morning and offered them to Maggie when she greeted them at the door.

"How nice of you, but you shouldn't have bothered." Maggie took the cookies, then led Jen and Aaron to the family room adjoining the kitchen.

Although the house had been designed in Victorian style, the Higgins family had modernized it. The place radiated a homey quality rather than the stiff formality of her grandmother's house. Jen decided to borrow some of Maggie's decorating ideas.

"Where's Bobby?" Her son's transparent eagerness to see his friend nearly caused Jen to laugh.

"He's out back playing with Rufus."

"Mom, Rufus is such a great dog. I wish we had a dog like him."

" Why don't you just go out the back way," Maggie suggested.

Aaron was gone in a flash.

"Sit down," Maggie said. "Want something to drink?"

"No, I'm fine. We just had lunch before coming over."

The family room had thick dark orange carpeting that looked well with the Early American furnishings. Maggie seated herself on a rocking chair.

"I hope we're not taking advantage of you. Aaron loves coming here but I don't want you to feel put upon."

Maggie played with her dangling silver earrings. "Absolutely not. Bobby and Pam both get along well with Aaron. He's easy to have around. Unlike Bobby, Pam's a quiet kid. Aaron draws her into their games." Maggie tossed her head of dark brown curls. "Pam's introverted while Bobby's an extrovert. They don't always get on well. But Aaron's good with both of them."

"I think it's because he's an only child. He's used to spending most of his time with adults, like I did when I was that age. But Aaron really loves being with other children. So this is great for him too."

Jen wondered if she should confide in Maggie about the problems she was having. But the topic seemed too unpleasant to dwell on. So they talked about the school system, exchanged recipes, and altogether passed an enjoyable afternoon discussing inconsequential matters. Maggie showed an interest in hearing about New York City. Jen obliged her by describing the tourist attractions and the fashion scene.

"Are you interested in getting a pet for Aaron?"

Jen was thoughtful. "I'm not certain. I've never had one."

"And we've always had so many," Maggie said.

"I guess Eric tries to find homes for a great many animals."

"He does. So many are abused or abandoned. Your grandmother was very generous in supporting our efforts."

Jen wasn't certain how to respond to that. She sensed she and Maggie could become good friends, and yet because of all the things that had happened to her, Jen was feeling suspicious and uncertain.

By the time she took Aaron home, her son was still in good spirits.

"Don't forget to bring your friend next time you come," Maggie said. "She's welcome too."

"Thank you. Maryann's been working all day at her computer."

After they got settled in the car, Aaron turned to her. "Mom, you're humming."

"Was I?" She hadn't noticed.

"You never hum anymore."

"Seeing you enjoy playing with your friends put me in a good mood." She gave Aaron a quick hug.

Jen looked for Maryann when they got back to the house. She found her friend upstairs in her room gazing off in space.

"I know you'll find another position soon."

Her friend's smile did not reach her deep green eyes. "I hope you're right."

"Of course, I am." Jen marched across the room and gave Maryann a hug just as she had earlier with Aaron.

"There's more. When Rob worked here this morning, we talked a little. I think he's interested in having a real relationship."

"And that upsets you?"

"It does. Common sense dictates any involvement with him would be stupid."

"Then again, feelings aren't necessarily sensible. I think it was Albert Einstein who said that common sense isn't common."

"I suppose."

"Would you help me fix dinner?"

That got her friend moving. Jen had discovered long ago that doing basic domestic things like cooking and cleaning took a person's mind off problems.

The doorbell rang just as Jen was about to place the chicken breasts into the oven to bake. Jen washed her hands and hurried to the door as Maryann pricked the red bliss potatoes and yams, turned them over, and placed them back in the oven.

Grant Coleman stood there, hands fisted in his pants pockets. "Sorry to bother you this late but I wanted to check on the surveillance cameras, make sure they're working properly."

He went about his task and Jen hurried back to the kitchen. "Grant Coleman's here to make certain those cameras are working."

"Do you want to ask him to stay for dinner?"

"I'll ask. But I doubt that he would be willing. Still we can just throw a couple of more chicken breasts on the pan. Worst that happens is we make chicken salad tomorrow."

"Would you care to stay for dinner? We've got plenty."

"That's a generous offer. But I generally eat supper over at the diner."

"I can offer you a healthier meal."

"All right," he said. He was rewarded by a big, bright smile that turned her face into a radiant sun.

"We really need to talk about a few things."

"After dinner? All right?"

He gave an abrupt nod. No sense ruining her supper.

Chapter Thirty-Two

"Good food," Grant Coleman said looking to Jen. His eyes lingered on her face.

"I hope you left room for dessert."

Grant let out a groan. "I have to let out my belt as it is."

Aaron jumped up. "You're gonna like the dessert though. It's the best part of the meal. I wouldn't eat all those vegetables if it wasn't for the dessert."

"Oh, really?" Jen placed her hands on her hips and gave her son a hard look.

Aaron lowered his eyes. "Well, I might eat some of them anyway. They don't taste so bad."

Jen had served a tossed salad with olives, chick peas, baby carrots, and small tomatoes besides cooked summer squash and broccoli. The chicken breasts, tender and juicy, had been baked just right with a hint of red wine for flavor. Grant had eaten with a hearty appetite.

"Okay, what's for dessert?"

"We do a special fresh fruit cocktail with a large dollop of vanilla fudge frozen yogurt."

He frowned at her. "Frozen yogurt?"

"It tastes just as good as ice cream," Aaron said. "Honor bright. Mom makes it special."

"Let's let Chief Coleman be the judge," she said to her son. Turning to Grant, she spoke again. "You decide. If you don't like it, I promise not to be offended, but I can't vouch for Maryann."

"Attacking a police officer is a capital offense." He offered a teasing smile.

Jen served the dessert and Grant admitted to enjoying it. "Rob's going to be awfully jealous if and when he finds out how well I've been treated here."

She looked over at Maryann. "We'll have to make it up to him. You've both been wonderful. Your mother and sisters are great too."

"Nice of you to say. I know you didn't always feel that way."

She turned her head sideways, not certain what to make of that remark. She wanted to question him about it when the phone rang and distracted her.

Aaron sprang to his feet. "I'll get it."

A moment later, Aaron shouted for her to pick up the phone. It turned out to be someone soliciting donations for a local charity. When she got off the phone, Jen told the others about the call.

"That brings up another reason I wanted to talk to you this evening," Grant said.

She and Maryann exchanged looks.

"Say Aaron, don't you have a video game you want to play with me?"

"Sure, but don't you have to clean up first?" Maryann said.

"Since your mom has company, we'll tackle it later. Bet I can beat you."

"Bet you can't." They raced each other upstairs, laughing all the way.

"She's good with him."

"Maryann likes children."

"I wouldn't expect that from a career woman."

"Most people are complex, not all one thing or another."

"You got me there."

They walked into the living room. He seated himself on a chair and she took one of the sofas.

"So what did you want to talk about?" Jen folded her hands together not certain what to expect.

"A couple of things, or should I say people." Grant leaned forward. "That friend of your mother's has a rap sheet."

Jen sat up straighter. "What does that mean exactly?"

"He's done some time. Not for violent crimes—that we know about. But Franklin Kraulley is a big question mark just the same."

Jen's eyes met his. "Do you think my mother's involved?"

"If Kraulley's responsible."

Jen licked dry lips. "My mother threatened to sue over the estate. She said she'd question my grandmother's mental competence at the time the new will was drawn up. I guess her case would be that much stronger if I moved out of the house and left town."

"Makes sense. I'll bring him in for questioning."

"I guess so. It's just so awful."

He got up and moved close then pulled Jen to her feet. "What would really be awful is if this person went further."

"You mean tried to kill me?"

"I'm sorry, but yes, that is what I mean."

"I'll never understand how people can deliberately harm others." She hugged her body feeling suddenly cold in spite of the warmth of the room.

"Some of them are sick."

"I'd say anyone who can plan to kill other people has to be mentally deranged."

"The main reasons or motives for murder are profit, revenge and jealousy. There are some people that would profit from your death. I plan to make certain that doesn't happen."

"Thank you. That's very reassuring. Since I don't plan on leaving town, I especially appreciate your help." She hesitated but then decided to offer her hand.

He took her hand and shook it, but then held it a few seconds longer before releasing her fingers. "That's just part of my job."

The living room was growing darker, shadows forming. She turned on one of the antique lamps which gave the room a soft glow.

"My mother and her boyfriend aren't the only possibilities, are they? Didn't you mention you were checking out the charities that inherit if I don't remain here?"

"I did." He met her gaze. "This Forrest Foundation is puzzling. All the other charities seem to check out. But I'm not so certain about that one. I'm going to talk with Forrest.

I'll have to handle him with care. He's ingratiated himself with some of the people in local politics like the mayor."

"And that makes a difference?"

He stared at her as if she were naïve. "Mrs. Stoddard…"

"Jen please."

He gave her a nod. "Jen, the police chief is appointed by the mayor. I believe I've served Bloomingvale well and that my record of service speaks for itself. However, I don't want this Forrest character running to the mayor crying harassment. So I'll take it slow and keep investigating."

"What if he contacts me again?"

"I don't think he will, not directly anyway."

She emitted a soft sound of pain.

"I'm just afraid of what will happen next. Maybe I am being foolish. Maybe I should give up and go back to New York. I want to stay here, to provide for my son's future, but at what cost?"

"You made a good decision. Stick with it. Don't change your mind now. I'm not going to let anything happen to you."

For a moment, he embraced her. Then as if he'd realized what he'd done, Grant pulled away. "It's going to be all right."

"I hope so."

"Better get going."

She walked him to the front door.

"Don't forget to lock up."

"Hey, I'm a New Yorker." She smiled at him.

His eyes lingered on hers. But then he turned away. She felt a sense of loss.

After Grant left, she walked around the house silent as a ghost. Should she just go back to New York? He'd promised to protect her but he couldn't be around all the time. And she couldn't afford a professional bodyguard, not that she would want one even if she could. She valued her privacy. Still, her grandmother wanted her to have this house and her estate. Grandmother trusted her to take care of what she left behind, and she'd felt Jen would have a better life here. To leave now would be to betray that trust. No, she would stay. She wouldn't run away cowering in fear from some shadowy malevolent antagonist.

Jen walked through the dining room and put on the light switch. Overhead the antique silver and crystal chandelier shone brightly. What could it tell her about the elegant dinners once served here? She ran her hands along the mahogany table that showed nary a scratch. Clearly it had been lovingly polished over the years. They had never eaten in this room. She vowed someday they would, on a day of celebration, a special occasion. Would there ever be such a day?

Chapter Thirty-Three

Rob observed that the grass looked dried out. It hadn't rained in several weeks. Farmers needed the rain for their crops. This was an area that grew corn, wheat, oats and soy. Farmers had come to town complaining about the lack of rain. The thought of losing their farms because of drought always sent fear into their hearts.

Rob thought about his father who had grown up on a farm with his family. After Rob's grandfather died, they'd lost the farm. His dad had been forced to drop out of school needing to help support the family. He'd gone to work in a factory. Eventually, he had gotten married and had children of his own. But the factory had shut down. His father explained how they'd found it was cheaper to relocate the factory where labor was cheaper and no unions existed.

Rob knew his father always wanted to go back to farming. He'd dreamed of owning his own land. But that never happened. He hired out to one place and then another. They'd finally come to town and he'd worked as a handyman. It hadn't been a good life and Dad took to drinking to forget his disappointments. His mother had been the backbone of the family. When his father floundered, she'd taken on the burden of responsibility for supporting their family.

Rob hoped to have his own family one day and do a lot better for them. Every time he saw Maryann Waller his heart ached. She sparkled like a star. But she was too good for him. He really had nothing much to offer her. If she married, it would likely be to some rich city guy, a fellow who drove an expensive car and wore a designer suit to work each day. She'd be gone soon anyway. He shouldn't even be thinking about her. Yet whenever he saw Maryann, all he could think about was how much he wanted to be with her.

He got out of his pick-up truck intending to walk over to the bank to deposit some checks when he saw Maryann sauntering toward the post office. She wore that floral sundress he'd seen her in before, the one that hugged her trim figure and made her look like a flower in full bloom. The sunlight brought the gold out in her hair.

"Hey, beautiful lady, how are you doing today?"

"I'm fine." She gave him a big smile, flashing pearly white teeth.

"Everything okay at the Pritchard house?"

"Good for now. Are you headed for the post office?"

"No, I'm going to the bank, but I'll walk you over."

They strolled together side by side as Rob tried to think of something to say to her. He wasn't usually at a loss for words.

"You know there's a Labor Day picnic sponsored by the town. It's a tradition around here. People come in from all around. It's a lot of fun. Think you'd like to go with me?"

"Would it be a problem if Jen and Aaron came too?"

He liked Mrs. Stoddard and her son. So he agreed and told Maryann he'd get back to her about the time and other information. "It's almost lunchtime," he said. "Why don't we eat together?"

She hesitated for a moment. "I guess we could. I have some letters to mail and then I'm free."

"Diner all right?"

Maryann wrinkled her nose. "I kind of like The Red Pepper better."

"Red Pepper it is."

"Gosh, you're a hard man to deal with."

"You better believe it."

They laughed together. He loved the way she laughed. Maybe he should tell her what was on his mind and see what her response might be. Maybe he'd take a gamble and roll the dice.

Maryann slammed into the house. She found Jen in the living room. Jen sat on a chair reading the novel she'd bought at the local bookstore. She looked up.

"Something wrong?"

"Rob Coleman."

"Oh." Jen closed her book, uncurled herself from her chair, and stood up. "Was he rude?"

"No." Maryann frowned.

"Nasty in some way?"

"No."

"What did he do that you consider so upsetting?"

"He wants me to stay in Bloomingvale. Now how can I possibly do that?" She plopped down on a sofa.

"Do you want to stay here? Because you know you're more than welcome."

Maryann burst into tears. "That's not the point. Don't you see? He's got me crazy."

Jen sat down beside her and put her arms around her. "He can't make you do anything you don't want to do. He's entitled to an opinion. It's obvious to me that he cares about you, and I'm not talking merely friendship here. And you're just as attracted to him, aren't you?"

Maryann nodded, feeling miserable. "He asked me to go with him to the Labor Day picnic the town sponsors. It appears to be a big community event."

"Are you going?"

"I said yes, but I told him only if you and Aaron go with us."

Jen let out a deep sigh. "I wish you hadn't done that. I think it's best if the two of you are alone. You need to sort things out, don't you?"

"No, we don't. I'm going back to New York after the holiday. I've finally got an excellent interview set up and I'll get that job or one equally as good. Rob Coleman has no place in my life."

"You're sure of that?"

Maryann raised her chin. "Absolutely and positively certain."

"Then, my dear, why are tears running down your face?"

She had no answer for Jen's question.

Chapter Thirty-Four

Burt Russell led Frank Kraulley into Grant's office. It appeared as if the two men had been involved in a physical altercation. They were both breathing hard and Burt had cuffed Kraulley.

"Am I being arrested for something? I didn't do nothing. You hick town cops are certifiable."

"Burt, please remove the handcuffs from Mr. Kraulley. Have a seat, sir."

"No thanks. I got nothing to say to you."

"That's all right because I have a few things to say and I think you better listen."

Kraulley's face had been bruised and his nose was bloody.

"Burt, how did Mr. Kraulley get battered?"

"When I asked him to come with me, he tried to punch me. Chief, I had to defend myself."

Grant gave a quick nod, pulled some tissues from a box on his desk and handed them to Kraulley. He surveyed the man who looked to Grant like a small time thug. He wondered how Sara Morrow had ever hooked up with him. She, who'd been such a social snob in her salad days.

"I have a few questions for you, Mr. Kraulley. We're not arresting you for anything. This is informal. However, if you want to have a lawyer present, that's you're right. Do you understand?"

"Sure, no lawyer. Not now anyway."

"Okay. Are you harassing Jennifer Stoddard?"

"What? Me? No. I don't know anything about that." Kraulley's eyes opened wide.

"Sara Morrow's angry at her daughter. She tell you about that?"

Kraulley slumped down in his chair. "Yeah, sure. I mean she's got every right. Her daughter gets the inheritance that should be hers. Who wouldn't be angry?"

Grant leaned over setting his sharp metallic gaze on Kraulley. "She'd want revenge. You being her good friend, you'd help her get even with her daughter, wouldn't you?"

Kraulley rose to his feet. "Me? No way. I got nothing to do with it."

"So you wouldn't threaten Mrs. Stoddard? I got that right? Would you take a lie detector test to prove it?"

Kraulley's eyes settled on the floor. "I don't have to do that. I didn't do anything wrong. Anyway, Sara's going to fight her daughter for the old lady's property all legal and proper in court. She's got a lawyer picked out already, a good one."

"So you wouldn't write threatening notes for instance or slash Mrs. Stoddard's tires?"

Kraulley kept his head down. "I told you. I didn't do anything to her. I don't need to do nothing because Sara's taking it to court. Now unless you're arresting me, I want to leave here."

"You have outstanding ticket violations."

"In Chicago, not here."

"You so much as spit on the sidewalk in this jurisdiction and you go to jail." Grant felt a hard line was needed in dealing with Kraulley to make a point.

"Seems I'm the one being harassed. So either read me my rights and I'll lawyer up, or let me go. Like the old saying goes, a fish can only be caught if it opens its mouth."

Grant looked at Burt and gave him a nod. The policeman escorted Kraulley from his office.

Grant went out to the squad room later and found Burt writing up a report. "So what did you think of Kraulley?"

Burt looked up at him, thick brown hair unruly as ever. "Can't say if he was lying or not. Did you mean it when you asked if he'd take a lie detector test?"

Grant shrugged. "Nope. We both know the results are inadmissible in court. So it would be a waste of time and money. A lot of these guys are sociopaths. We likely wouldn't even get an accurate reading. Someone like Kraulley probably lies all the time. I just wanted to see his reaction."

Grant felt frustrated. He seemed to be getting nowhere in finding out who attempted to harm Jennifer Stoddard. If it was a matter of revenge, Sara Morrow had a good motive. But would she hurt her own daughter? Maybe. Grant felt the woman had a ruthless nature. And the boyfriend likely had few scruples.

Still, Grant realized he needed solid proof not mere supposition. There had been a small blood sample on the broken cellar window. He'd be able to compare DNA. He went back to his office and collected the discarded tissue with blood from Kraulley's nose. Hopefully, it would be enough to use for a comparison.

Jen wondered why Rob Coleman had come by the house. Was he looking for Maryann? If so, she doubted that her friend would be pleased. Regardless, she greeted him with a warm smile.

"Hot out there today." He swiped at his forehead with a blue bandana.

"Come in and I'll get you a cold drink."

Aaron came running to see who had arrived at the door. "Hi, Rob. My friends are coming over later today."

"That's great. Have fun." Rob lifted Aaron in the air and her son laughed, pleased by the attention. "How's the air up there?"

"I like it better on the ground."

Rob put Aaron back on his feet.

Jen waited for Rob to explain the reason for his visit since she hadn't been expecting him.

"I hate being the bearer of bad tidings, but I found something you need to know about."

Jen felt a sense of alarm sweep over her. "What is it?"

"Well, it's something we can fix."

"Go on."

"There's termites and also carpenter ants."

"Oh, no!"

"They're feasting on your wooden beams. Need to do some repair work there. The good news is this is very recent and so there's no real damage as yet."

Aaron wrinkled his nose. "Can I see them?"

"Sure. We'll go down to the cellar."

"Wow, are they really eating our wood? Is there other stuff down there too?" Aaron's eyes were large with interest.

"Well, I did find some spiders and then there were a couple of snakes." He saw Jen's expression. "Just some small green garden snakes that managed to crawl in. They're not dangerous."

"Snakes," Aaron repeated. "Cool."

"That's a matter of opinion," she said in a dry voice.

"I can get an exterminator in whenever you like." Rob's efforts to reassure her weren't helping.

She nibbled her lower lip. "We'd have to get out for a few days. When Maryann leaves for New York, I'll arrange for Aaron and myself to stay over at the inn. It shouldn't be crowded after Labor Day."

"Sounds like a plan. I'll set things up so we can fix the problem. One or two of the wooden support beams were weakened by the insects so I'll take care of that after the extermination." He flashed her an encouraging smile. "It'll be fine."

She sighed.

"It seems like there's always something that needs to be repaired in this place."

Rob nodded his agreement. "That's the nature of old houses. They're money pits. But this place is worthy of the restoration. It's got fine lines, excellent architecture."

"I don't disagree. Speaking of which, I need suggestions as to who can refinish some of the old furniture."

"Not a problem. I know some good people."

At that moment, Maryann ambled down the staircase. When she saw Rob, her friend stopped abruptly, almost tripping.

"Rob came by to tell us we have termites."

"I'm sorry."

"I think we all are."

"Not me," Aaron said. "I want to go see them."

"If you must," she said.

"I'll show them to Bobby later. He'll think they're cool too."

Chapter Thirty-Five

The Forrest Foundation was located at the edge of town in a large white clapboard building. Grant climbed the stairs and entered the house with agility. Seated at a desk near the door, a receptionist answered a ringing phone. She didn't notice him at first.

Grant didn't mind. The fact that she happened to be busy gave him an opportunity to look around. The receiving area had tasteful furnishings, the room decorated in shades of beige. Soft music piped in. Large poster photos of appealing children covered the walls. The children, boys and girls of many nationalities and races, were malnourished and clothed in rags. Strong emotional appeal.

The woman at the desk finished her phone call and turned to him. "Can I help you?" Her manner was polite and perfunctory. She was middle-aged, chubby, frizzy-haired and wore bifocals. The sign on her desk read: Mrs. Patricia Kraft.

"I'm Grant Coleman, Police Chief in Bloomingvale. I'm looking for Mr. Forrest."

"Mr. Forrest is busy at the moment. Would you like to make an appointment to see him?" Her tone registered much cooler now that she knew he wasn't a prospective donor.

"I think Mr. Forrest will see me," Grant's tone matched hers. "I'm here in regard to the donations Mrs. Pritchard made to his charity."

Patricia Kraft adjusted her eyeglasses and picked up her phone. She buzzed Forrest, explaining who was waiting to see him. Forrest strode to the receiving area from behind a closed door in record time.

He offered a handshake. "Chief, how nice to meet you. Mayor Longworth speaks highly of you. I always trust her judgment regarding people."

"Good to know."

"Patricia said you've come to make inquiries? Something about Mrs. Pritchard's donations to the Forrest Foundation?"

Grant studied the man. Forrest reminded him of a white rat. His ruddy face, white hair, short posture and large mid-section made the man appear harmless. But Grant's gut instinct told him Forrest was not the genial older gentleman he appeared to be.

"I think we ought to talk in your office."

"Certainly." Forrest turned to the woman at the desk. "Patricia, hold my calls for now please." With that, he led Grant through to the office area.

Grant gave a quick look around. The upstairs looked as if it were designated as living quarters. Not a bad setup. Forrest's office appeared meant to impress. Bookcases lined the walls. The books had leather bindings. The desk had a gold letter opener sitting on it. A far cry from his own Spartan office.

"Now you were saying?"

"You visited Jennifer Stoddard when she moved into her grandmother's house."

Forrest viewed him askance out of the corner of his eye. "That's right I did."

"You requested she continue giving funds to your charity as her grandmother did."

"Again, that's correct. I find that the families of my contributors generally like to continue to make donations in honor of their relatives who have passed on. I assumed Mrs. Stoddard would want to follow her grandmother in that tradition. But of course she is perfectly free to do as she chooses."

Grant narrowed his eyes. "You gave her a hard sell. I think she told you that she doesn't have the money right now to make any large donations."

Forrest swiveled in his chair. "Of course, I understand that completely."

Grant leaned over the desk. "Do you? Because you see someone's been harassing Mrs. Stoddard, trying to frighten her. I want to make sure you had nothing to do with it."

Forrest got to his feet. "I can assure you that I am a reputable man and I run a reputable charity. I do not harass anyone." His face had turned a mottled purple color.

"Glad to hear it. Because you know there are a lot of crooked scams out there that claim to be legit charities. Tell me, Mr. Forrest, how much of the money that you collect goes to feeding and clothing those orphans? What percentage ends up in your pocket?"

"Naturally there are administrative fees. That's true of all charities." Forrest gave a nervous glance at his watch. "Chief, you must excuse me now. I'm expecting someone. Perhaps another time? That is, if you have more questions. Please give Mrs. Stoddard my regards."

"I'll be sure to do that."

"Her grandmother was a wonderful woman. Kind, generous to a fault." The smile he wore was pasted on, probably as phony as Grant suspected his charity to be.

Grant turned to Mrs. Kraft back in the entry area. "Could you hand me some of the brochures for The Forrest Foundation?"

"How many pieces of the literature would you like?" She gave him a lopsided smile, looking a tad nervous.

"Just one of each."

"Would you perhaps be thinking of making a contribution to our cause?"

Now it was his turn to smile. He took the leaflets she handed him and left without answering her question.

Chapter Thirty-Six

Jen frowned as she went over her finances. The house really was a money pit. So much still should be done. Rob's verdict on the roof had been discouraging. He'd patched it for the time being, but a new roof would be needed eventually, maybe even before the snowstorms of winter hit the heartland. The money allocated for repair and maintenance of the house had seemed ample initially but the funds were dwindling. She would talk to Mr. Donne. She didn't look forward to it though. Financial matters had never been her forte.

"You're looking worried. Something wrong?"

Jen glanced up at Maryann. "It's my financial situation. I'm having some problems sorting things out."

Maryann pulled up a chair beside her at the desk in the study. "What sort of problems? Maybe I can help."

"That would be wonderful. I would appreciate your expertise."

"Well, I admit I wasn't all that great in accounting which was why I got my M.B.A. in business administration. But I know a little."

"Would you be available today if I can get Mr. Donne to see us?"

"Of course. I'll help in any way I can."

"Then there's no time like the present." Jen found the lawyer's card in the desk drawer and dialed his number. She felt edgy but wasn't certain why.

Mr. Donne's assistant picked up on the third ring. Jen explained her reason for the call.

"We're just back from vacation," Astra Meyers said. "Mr. Donne has quite a few appointments today. Can this wait?"

Usually Jen would have agreed to postpone the meeting. She was not by nature an assertive person. But Maryann wouldn't be here much longer. Difficult as it was, she insisted on a meeting as soon as possible. Astra reluctantly fitted her in for a late afternoon appointment.

"Thank you for seeing me today," Jen said.

"Well, as I told you, Mrs. Stoddard, my sister's son, Edward Norris, does all of our accounting work. He's a C.P.A. and an auditor." Donne turned to Maryann. "And who might this young lady be?"

"Maryann is my friend and has an M.B.A. in business. I thought her presence might be helpful."

"Of course." Mr. Donne gave her a patrician nod.

Maryann simply smiled politely at the attorney.

"The truth is that I'm confused about a few things and I wanted some clarification. Maybe we should be talking to your nephew since,as you suggest, he knows the most about the financial state of my grandmother's estate." Jen kept her tone polite but she had no intention of backing down. She vowed Mr. Donne would not intimidate her.

He, in turn, frowned at her. "What is it that you wish to know? Perhaps I can be of some assistance." He leaned forward in his chair, his wrinkled face like a pattern of mosaic tile, his stooped posture more evident.

"To start with, the house needs more repairs then we initially realized. The money set aside probably won't cover all of it. My own personal finances are rather limited at present. Is more money available from the estate?"

He gave her a sympathetic look. "I'm afraid not. It's all invested. Edward could explain that better than I can."

"When might we talk to him? Can it be today while Maryann is still in town?"

Mr. Donne appeared taken aback. "I doubt that would be possible."

"Could you please give me his phone number and address? His office is nearby–am I correct?"

"Well, yes, but that isn't the way things are usually done."

"Mr. Donne, this is very important to me."

"All right, I will see what I can do for you." He sounded annoyed but she wasn't going to back down. This was too important.

"Now. Please."

After they left the lawyer's office, Maryann turned to her. "Jen, I've never seen you so forceful."

"Was I rude? I hope not. I didn't mean to be."

Maryann placed her hand on Jen's shoulder. "No, you handled him just right. I'm impressed."

"But it does seem hopeless."

Maryann shrugged. "Let's go visit Mr. Norris and see what he has to say. Nothing's set in stone as far as I can see."

Jen referred to the business card Mr. Donne had given her and dialed his nephew's phone number on her cell. She got to speak with his assistant and explained the urgent need for an appointment. The assistant slotted her for an hour hence. Jen breathed a sigh of relief. She gave a thumbs up sign to Maryann who smiled and nodded her approval.

The accountant's office turned out to be in Hardin, two towns away and a good drive. Jen still didn't feel comfortable driving any distance, but since Maryann sat beside her, the trip turned out to be more pleasant than intimidating.

Edward Norris appeared to be waiting for them. No one else frequented his office. He probably intended to go home early. Summer hours. Well, he would have to wait on that.

He shook hands with them both. Jen noted that his hand felt damp. Was he perspiring? The office seemed well air-conditioned. He invited them to sit down.

Jen studied the man. He had thick, sandy brows and a mustache to match. His hair looked styled rather than merely cut. His suit appeared well-cut and expensive. His fingernails had been manicured. He had a good tan as if he'd vacationed recently on a beach somewhere. The accountant obviously did well for himself.

"Now how can I help you?"

"I'm certain your uncle told you," Jen said. "So I'll get to the bottom line. Is there more money available for the house? There are additional repairs needed. I will require more cash."

Norris frowned at her. "I'm afraid that isn't possible. When you legally come into possession of the house and your grandmother's assets, matters will be different."

Jen took a deep breath and let it out slowly to calm herself. "Mr. Norris, I would like to see the estate records. I would like to know specifically what my grandmother had in assets at the time of her death."

Norris rose to his feet. "I believe you have a copy of the will. You are not entitled to any further assets until you inherit your grandmother's property. That will not occur for approximately two more years. Your grandmother made no provision for additional funds other than what you have already received. Now, ladies, you'll have to excuse me. I have an important appointment elsewhere. I only saw you today as a courtesy to my uncle." His manner had changed from polite to unfriendly and downright hostile. He hurried them out of his office.

She exchanged a look with Maryann. Her friend's expression indicated a similar reaction.

"What do you think?"

Maryann shook her head. "Challenging people about money sometimes brings out the worst in them. But he could be hiding something."

Jen sighed as they walked back to the car. "He acted as if it were his money I asked for. Sorry to waste your time."

"We'll work on this together." Maryann's sunny, reassuring smile made her feel much better.

Chapter Thirty-Seven

Maryann felt terrible about leaving Bloomingvale. It did appear to be a pleasant place to live. She especially hated to leave Jen and Aaron. She recognized that Jen's unfinished business here would benefit from her knowledge and expertise. But in a week, she needed to be headed back to New York for her interview.

Unwanted came the vision of Rob Coleman looking at her with those earnest eyes. Those eyes haunted her. No man had ever looked at her the way he did. And he was such an attractive man, not just physically, although he certainly appealed on that level. But there seemed to be an innate goodness in the man, a kindness, you didn't often see. Strange how she hardly noticed his limp anymore. It didn't really matter.

She shook her head trying to clear her mind. Thoughts of Rob Coleman would do her no good. She must go back to preparing for interviews in New York. Another corporation had answered her query. They were going to schedule an interview for the same week too. She would be very busy.

A light tap at the door of the room caught her attention.

"Maryann, Rob came by. He wants to talk to you. Can you come down?"

"Be right there." Out of habit she went to the mirror, ran a comb through her hair and put on a fresh coat of lipstick. She caught herself about to change to a different outfit. Why would she bother? Why should she?

When she swept down the staircase, she found Rob standing there in the foyer. He looked hunky, dressed in jeans, T-shirt and a baseball cap. The well-worn clothes fit his muscled body to perfection.

"Hi, Rob, Jen said you came to see me?"

"Both of you really. I wanted to know if you want to participate in some of the activities for the Labor Day picnic. There's going to be some races like the three-legged race, best pie gets a blue ribbon, followed by a pie eating contest. It's all old-fashioned, good-natured fun. I just wanted to know if you'd like to go over the list with me and maybe sign up for something."

She gave him a dubious look. "I don't think so. I'd prefer to be a bystander. But please feel free to enter anything you like."

"Would you cheer me on?"

"Absolutely, I'm a great cheerleader."

He gave her a broad smile. "I bet you are. You sure you don't want to do the three-legged race with me?"

"I'm certain. But I know someone who'd love to sign up with you."

"And who would that be?"

She smiled back at him. "Aaron, of course. Although he's been spending most of his time with Bobby Higgins these days."

"I just keep losing out." Rob voice teased her.

Jen and Aaron came down the stairs, Aaron barreling along far in the lead of his mother.

"Hey, Rob. Are you working here today?"

"Not today, sport. Just came by with a schedule of activities for the Labor Day picnic. See if you want to sign up for anything." He removed a folded sheet of paper from his back pocket and handed it to Aaron.

"Cool!" The boy snatched it eagerly and began reading the document with interest. "There's a relay race and a hundred-yard dash. I bet Bobby and I could enter those. I'm going to take this over to Bobby's house."

"I'll walk you over," Jen said. "Wait for me."

Jen turned to Rob. "I'm not certain when I'll have more work for you to do on the house. I'd like to renovate the rest of the rooms upstairs, but right now it isn't possible."

"No problem."

Jen hurried after her son, leaving Maryann alone with Rob.

He turned back to her. "Did I take you away from something important?"

She shook her head. "I was working on my Q and A."

"Your what?"

"Questions and answers for my interviews. I try to generate every conceivable question I could be asked by the corporate team. Then I write up answers, go over them, practice in front of a mirror."

Rob shook his head. "Why go to so much trouble?"

"It's really necessary if you want to appear well-informed. I always do lots of research on a company and its products before I interview with them."

"Suppose you get thrown completely different questions than what you expect?"

She shrugged. "Then I have to improvise, wing it. I can manage. I have in the past. But I still believe it's important to be fully prepared. I think it was Napoleon who said that luck occurs when preparation meets opportunity."

"Did he say that before or after Waterloo?"

"Very funny. Do you take anything seriously?"

"Could be you over-think things. Doesn't pay to worry."

She found herself getting annoyed with him. "When men are hardworking and ambitious, they're admired. Women get criticized."

He frowned and placed his hand on her arm. She felt that frisson of awareness that so unsettled her. "I didn't mean to insult you. I admire you more than you could know. I just meant to say that you need to relax and enjoy life more. Tomorrow will take care of itself."

She folded her arms together. "That's the difference between us. I guess I'm a pessimist while you're an optimist."

"We can agree to disagree and still be friends, can't we?" His voice coaxed her.

"Is that what you want, for us to be friends?"

"I'll take what I can get." He moved closer to her and ran his hand along her cheek in a soft caress.

"I better get back to my Q and A."

"You just do that. So no games or activities for you at the picnic?"

"Afraid not. I'll just be a spectator."

"Coward." There was a glint in his eye.

"That's me. I don't intend to make a fool of myself."

"You couldn't if you tried." His eyes ran over her and she felt her blood begin to heat.

His lips were inches from her own. She wanted him to kiss her. She wanted to melt in his arms. But that was insane. She didn't belong with him. She shook off the feelings of want and hurried away from Rob.

A loud knock at his door jolted Grant. "Come in," he called out.

Mayor Longworth burst into his office. The pants suit she wore served to accentuate her tall, gaunt frame. At the moment, she bore down on Grant with a Medusa-like stare that could have turned lesser men to stone.

"I just came from having a very disturbing talk with one of our constituents."

He sat back in his chair. "Let me guess, that wouldn't be Samuel Forrest, would it?"

"That man is a large campaign contributor. He's one of the people who keep me in office, which in turn means he keeps you working as police chief."

Hands on hips, toe tapping against the floor, the mayor did not look as if she could be easily placated. Grant decided not to bother trying.

"I've been looking into Forrest's charity. Just so you know, the Forrest Foundation seems fishy. CharityWatch, CharityNavigator and Forbes regularly publish charity ratings. A small percentage of the money that Forrest takes in appears to actually go for those poor orphans. I can investigate further."

"No, please don't do that." Now she appeared to be on the defensive. Good. He'd given her something to think about.

"Word to the wise. If I were a politician, I'd disassociate myself from a guy like Forrest. Eventually, it will come back to bite you in the derriere."

The mayor's face reddened. She left the office slamming the door behind her.

Chapter Thirty-Eight

Jen had the unique experience of having the afternoon to herself. Maryann decided to work in her room at her laptop. Aaron had gone swimming again with Bobby and the Higgins family. It should please her being given this time to relax. But being alone didn't make her happy. Jen found things were best for her when she kept busy, otherwise she tended to worry.

She still had no clue what she would do once Aaron went off to school and Maryann returned to New York. Some women had useful talents. They could turn hobbies into occupations, become artists, writers, chefs, clothing designers. She couldn't even clean homes with the skill Linda Coleman and her daughters managed to do. True, she happened to be well-educated, but so were a great many other women. She wondered about going back to school, taking required education courses and getting certified as a science teacher. But she knew herself to be a shy person. Could she manage to control a class of exuberant children? Probably not. Perhaps library work would suit her. However, with a poor economy, library jobs were also scarce. Where was her life headed? She couldn't say, had no clue. Other than being the best possible mother she could be to Aaron, she felt unsure of herself.

Maybe now would be a good time to look closely at the rooms that she had been ignoring, although remodeling them for the time being seemed like a remote possibility. Still, there were probably some simple improvements she could manage to make on her own. If nothing else, it would give her some sense of accomplishment which she needed.

Her grandmother's room came to mind. It had been the master bedroom and as such had at some point been renovated to include its own bathroom. Jen's decision to

143

leave it as it had been was based more on sentimentality than good sense.

She entered the room and tried to view it as a decorator would. Her eyes caught the faded rose pattern wallpaper. That needed to be stripped away and a fresh coat of paint applied as had been done downstairs. She was not a big fan of dated wallpaper.

There were still clothes in the closets. Most of them would need to be tossed out. Some could be donated to charity. It made her heart heavy, but she knew these were things that needed to be done. Today she would make a start, however painful.

Jen went to her grandmother's bureau drawer. Here too many items stared back at her, each with its own small memory. There were perfume vials, sundry small trinkets. All of these things reminded her of the wise, kind woman who had passed away. In the bottom of the drawer, she found an envelope. On the outside, she saw her name in large black letters: "For Jen." She blinked.

Her grandmother had left a note for her? She hadn't expected that. She opened it and began reading. The handwriting seemed spidery and hard to decipher as if the act of writing were a painful one done with arthritic fingers.

"My Dear Granddaughter,

If you are reading this, it probably means that I am no longer among the living. I want you to know that I have thought long and hard about my decision as to how I should allocate my worldly possessions. My jewelry is in a safety deposit box and will belong to your mother to do with as she chooses. By the time you read this, I'm certain she will already be in possession of those items. However, I want you to have my house and investments. I want to provide for you and my great grandson. I know that your husband's death has left you in difficult circumstances. I believe you will put our family assets to good use whereas your mother would only squander them.

Mr. Donne has my new will and knows my wishes. I will soon be in a care facility. I trust you will find this letter and know what to do with it. There is a safe that your grandfather had installed in this room many years ago. Use the numbers in my birthday as the combination. You will find the safe hidden behind your favorite painting

Jen observed that the Cezanne landscape print had been moved from its original location to another. She had often admired it and told her grandmother so. The print itself had no great intrinsic value other than its beauty to the eye of the beholder.

Jen removed the painting and found the safe underneath it just as her grandmother had described. The first time she tried putting in the numbers, it didn't seem to work. Had she been confused about her grandmother's date of birth? She doubted that. Had her grandmother made a mistake in setting the safe's combination. But no, Velma Pritchard possessed a clear, sharp mind. Jen doubted that would have deserted her grandmother even when her physical strength had. Jen tried again, and this time it worked. She heard the tumblers click into place, pulled the handle and the door to the safe opened.

She peered inside the safe. There were a number of papers. Birth certificates, death certificates. One document happened to be another signed copy of her grandmother's current will. Another large manila envelope had her name on the outside. She opened it and stared at a vast amount of cash. Her eyes opened wide. She located another note written in her grandmother's distinctive handwriting.

"Dearest Jennifer,

I have worried that the money I allocated for house maintenance will not be enough to sustain you until you inherit my property. Please use this cash as a discretionary fund for whatever you need. I hope it will be enough. I could only guess."

Jen sat down heavily on the bed. Grandmother in her wisdom must have realized that more money might be needed. How much had been set aside? Jen began to count out the funds. Most of the money appeared to be in twenty and ten dollar denominations. There were also a few fifties. She stared at the currency as if they were alien objects from another planet. In the end, she counted two hundred thousand dollars. This money would be more than enough to see her through the next two years. She had every intention of being frugal with it. She took the two personal notes from her grandmother, most of the money, and placed them back in the safe, locking it again and adjusting the Cezanne print over it. She would remove the money as needed. In the meantime, she took one thousand dollars in small bills to place in her own room, temporarily stuffing the money in the pockets of her jeans.

For no sensible reason she could discern, she burst into tears. She supposed they were tears of gratitude for her grandmother's thoughtfulness. At that moment, someone entered the room.

"Jen? Are you all right? I've been looking for you."

She wiped her eyes with the back of her hand. "I'm fine, Maryann. Just that being in my grandmother's room has been a bit overwhelming."

Maryann eyed her with a sympathetic expression. "Of course, I understand. If you'd prefer to be alone, just tell me."

"No, I'm fine." Should she tell her friend about her discovery? She wasn't sure. If Maryann accidentally told anyone, and Mr. Donne or his nephew found out, would they then demand that these additional funds were part of the estate and not hers to keep? But her grandmother made it clear in her notes that the money was intended for her expenses. Jen was torn. She had never been secretive. It wasn't her nature to be anything but open and honest with other people. Yet this matter confused her. She decided to share the information with Maryann if it ever became necessary. Not an easy decision, but for the moment, it seemed right.

"It's rather warm. I'm going to change into shorts and then we can decide about dinner. Aaron should be home soon."

"Great. I'll go downstairs and get things started." Maryann went off and Jen went to her bedroom.

She felt guilty, almost dishonest, as she stuffed the bills into her own dresser drawer.

After she changed to lighter clothing, Jen found Maryann boiling pasta.

"I thought we'd combine this with some fresh vegetables and a nice salad with herbs and cheese."

"Sounds like a perfect meal for a hot summer evening. I'll toast some of that good bread we bought at Bigelow's."

They worked together side by side for a time in congenial silence.

"I think Rob will miss you a great deal when you leave," Jen observed.

"He'll find another female fast enough. The women around here will want to snatch him. I think he just likes me because I offer him a challenge."

"I'm not so certain that's what he feels."

Maryann stopped working and turned to her. "I don't think I really want to know about that."

"You don't want him having serious feelings for you?"

"No, I don't."

Maryann's tone indicated the conversation made her uneasy. Jen didn't pursue it. Maybe there were things even friends shouldn't discuss.

Chapter Thirty-Nine

Grant studied the list of charities Astra Meyers had provided. Maybe he ought to have a chat with Dr. Kramer. It seemed unthinkable that someone like Dr. Gus would harm anyone. Yet the fact remained that his free clinic would benefit if Jennifer Stoddard left town. There seemed to be a lot of money at stake. People had killed for less.

Abby Kramer sat at the front desk in the doctor's office. Grant knew the doctor's wife acted as his receptionist, bookkeeper and general majordomo.

"Hi, Chief. What can we do for you?"

"My knee's been acting up. The old football injury's causing me some pain. Thought maybe the doc could squeeze me in today."

Abby shook her head apologetically. "Sorry, Chief, he's completely double-booked for today. How about an appointment for tomorrow, unless it's an emergency."

"No, it's not an emergency. I'll phone." He moved as if to leave but then turned around. "Say I just found out something I meant to ask about."

Abby's thin brows lifted. "What would that be?"

"Velma Pritchard donated a lot of money to your free clinic."

Abby stood up. She looked uncomfortable. "Oh that, yes, she tended to be philanthropic. We were very sorry when she passed away."

"Helped keep the clinic going, did she?"

"Chief, Gus provides free medical care every Saturday to anyone who needs it and might not otherwise be able to afford it. People come from far and near for those services. Ella helps out as well. Not everyone has money for health insurance. Mrs. Pritchard sympathized. She was a good woman."

Grant decided he ought to drop by and see Jennifer Stoddard and bring her up to speed on his progress, or rather lack of progress, on her case.

Her son greeted him at the door "The policeman's here, Mom." He made the announcement as his mother entered the hallway.

"So I see." She offered a gentle smile.

The boy looked up at him. "Do you have any children?"

"No, I don't."

The child looked disappointed. "How about a dog? Do you have one?"

"I did when I was a kid like you, but I don't now."

"Do you have any pets?"

"Sorry, no pets."

"That's all right. I don't have any either, but I'm going to try to convince Mom to let me get a puppy," the boy confided. "My friend Bobby's got a great big dog. They call him Rufus the Red. He's an Irish setter. He jumps on you and slobbers, but he's real friendly."

Jennifer looked embarrassed. "Chief, why don't you join me in the study? Aaron,

didn't you promise me you were going to clean your room before Bobby comes over?"

The boy hung his head and moaned. "Oh, Mom, Bobby doesn't care about stuff like that. His room isn't any neater than mine, and his mother doesn't make him clean up the mess."

"I'm sure she does have him put his toys away. Probably in the evening when you've already gone home."

"I could do it then too."

She let out an exasperated sigh. "Young man, go to your room please."

He wrinkled his freckled nose at her but climbed up the stairs without further comment.

"Cute kid," Grant commented as he followed Jennifer through the hall and down to a well-appointed study.

"He's getting to be a handful."

Grant didn't comment further, but a boy of that age needed a father. On the other hand, Grant reminded himself he'd had a father who'd been abusive. That hadn't worked out well at all.

"I wouldn't have fussed about Aaron cleaning his room, but I didn't want him listening in on our conversation."

He gave her a nod of understanding. He couldn't help but notice how attractive she looked. She still had a pretty face and a good figure. Even her voice pleased.

"First, have there been any further incidents? Anything done to your car?"

"No, nothing."

"How about the house? Has Rob been by to check on things?"

"It's been quiet around here this week. I haven't noticed anything out of the ordinary."

"That's good. I should tell you that I've spoken to both of the individuals we had some reason to consider persons of interest. I'm referring to your mother's pal Franklin Kraulley and Samuel Forrest of the Forrest Foundation."

Jennifer Stoddard leaned forward. "What did you tell them?"

"Just that someone has been harassing you. I asked if they knew anything about it."

"And did they?"

"They didn't admit to anything. I didn't expect they would. It was my way of giving them a warning to leave you alone."

She smiled at him. "I think it may have worked. Neither one of them has come by, and as I told you, nothing terrible has occurred this week."

He decided not to mention anything about Dr. Gus. He stood up. "Well, I hope that will be the end of it. But if anything happens, anything at all, don't feel embarrassed to contact me. If I'm not available for some reason, we have uniformed officers who are."

"Thank you. You've been wonderful." She touched his arm but then retracted it as if she'd touched a fire and burned herself.

Chapter Forty

Rob Coleman gulped down a bottle of water. He'd been putting new shingles on a house and the heat had finally gotten to him. He sat down in the shade of a big white oak tree and thought about the Labor Day picnic just a few days away. The thought of being with Maryann for the day brought him pleasure, but the knowledge that she'd be leaving town soon seared him with pain. He wanted to change her mind, just didn't see how that would be possible.

He thought about the situation again later when he had dinner with his family. His mother and sisters had finished their work early. In a cheerful manner, they joked around. Mentally, he withdrew into his own space.

"Rob, where are you?" His mother and sisters stared at him.

"What?"

"Mom asked you something. You looked like you were visiting another planet." His sister Lori threw him a speculative look.

"Just got some things on my mind."

"Are you still working on the Pritchard house?" His mother handed him a plate heaped with ham, beans and sweet potatoes.

"I'm done for now. But Mrs. Stoddard has plenty more that needs work there. Pretty sure she'll be contacting me again soon."

"She's a good customer for us too." Sue dug into her own plate with gusto. "I like her."

Grant entered the kitchen. "Who do you like?"

"Mrs. Stoddard. She's good to work for."

Rob saw a shadow cross his brother's face. "I wish you didn't work for her."

Their mother pushed back a lock of hair that had fallen across her forehead. "I don't understand what your problem is with her. She's a good person. Her mother, well, that's another story entirely. But Jennifer reminds me of her grandmother."

"I'm going to be taking her friend Maryann to the Labor Day picnic," Rob said. He could tell from Grant's expression that his brother didn't approve.

"You're making a mistake getting involved with her. Why don't you date a local girl?"

"You think she's too good for me?" Rob faced his brother.

Their mother, feeling the rising tension between her two sons, tried to move between them. "Nobody's too good for either one of you. Any woman would be downright lucky to have you boys interested in her."

Lori hooted. "Spoken like a loyal mother!"

"Not that you're prejudiced or anything," Sue teased.

Linda Coleman tossed a quelling look at her daughters. "All of my children are wonderful. Anyone who doesn't realize that isn't worthy of you. Now start eating. Dinner's getting cold."

Jen shopped at DeNuccio's that afternoon. Maryann had offered to keep an eye on Aaron and Bobby. So there was plenty of time to look around. She examined the fruits and vegetables with care. They all loved the variety of produce available at this time of the year. She would select the makings for a fine dinner salad.

"You like that kind of lettuce?"

Grant Coleman's deep voice startled her and she dropped the package of Mesclun she'd been holding. He bent down, scooped it up and handed it back to her.

"I didn't know you shopped here."

He shrugged. "Everyone in town does. But I don't eat much at my place. Just came in to pick up a sandwich at the appetizing counter."

"I haven't tried their prepared food. It does look good." She was aware they were talking like polite strangers. That probably was for the best. After all, they were strangers who hardly knew anything about each other.

"Yeah, good stuff here."

"I take it you don't cook?"

"I can, just prefer not to. So everything okay with you?" His tone sounded casual but his gaze expressed something quite different.

"Fine," she said.

"No more problems?"

Jen shook her head. Why did her heart start to race whenever she saw him? She wondered if he realized it. She hoped not.

"My brother tells me he's escorting you and your friend to the Labor Day picnic."

"Yes, we're all looking forward to it." She managed a small smile.

"Rob really likes your friend." His expression increased in intensity.

"Yes, I know that. I think Maryann has similar feelings for him."

"Does she?" He threw her a dubious look. "I'd hate for my brother to get hurt."

"So would I." She wanted to reassure him, but how could she when Maryann had expressed her intention of returning to the city on numerous occasions.

"She set to leave?"

Jen put the lettuce into her cart. "After Labor Day."

"My brother's hoping she'll change her mind. He's a bone deep optimist."

"But you're not?"

His eyes became steel. "Let's just say I've seen the darker side of humanity."

She thought a change of subject might be a good idea but what did they have in common?

"I guess we'll see you at the picnic."

"We'll be working there."

"Crowd control?"

"Right, and steering traffic. Whatever's needed. We keep an eye on the teenagers for instance. Sometimes they sneak beers and get rowdy."

"Will you get to enjoy the picnic?"

"Probably not."

"Well, make certain you visit us. We'll have lots of extra food for hard-working police officers."

"So will my mother and sisters." He clearly intended to keep his distance.

"I imagine your mother is a good cook."

"You imagine right. She's the best. Have a good time at the picnic."

"Thank you." She watched him walk away from her toward the appetizing counter. Why had it been so difficult for her to talk to him? But she knew the answer. Jen let out a deep sigh and tried her best to concentrate on her shopping. Other things were best forgotten.

Grant could have kicked himself. Why had he gone over and talked to her? He didn't even like the woman, did he? Just because she looked so delicate and feminine while selecting her produce? No, who was he kidding? There was just something about her that got to him. He hated it but couldn't seem to shake the need to be with her. Of course, if he was honest with himself, he would have to admit that he wanted to do a lot more than just talk to her. He felt like he was back in high school wanting to date her. And look how that had turned out? He shook his head and tried his best to clear any foolish thoughts about Jennifer Stoddard out of his head like cobwebs crowding a corner of his thick skull. He was a mature adult not a randy teenager: logic before lust.

Chapter Forty-One

Maryann enjoyed her afternoon with Aaron and Bobby. Jen would probably have let them run around happy by themselves, but she liked spending time with the children. First they played hide and seek together. That caused a lot of running around outside and figuring out hiding places. They laughed together when Maryann caught them or they caught her. It was great fun frolicking with them.

But at one point when Maryann had hidden near an old tool shed, she saw someone parked up the street in a silver Mercedes. She noted that the driver was a man. She might not have noticed him at all had he not slumped down behind the wheel as if to avoid being recognized. That troubled her.

Maryann observed that the man in the Mercedes sat up straighter when the boys ran out on the lawn. He appeared to be watching for them, or at least trying to do so. Why? And who was he? She resolved that she would tell Jen about this and let her decide what to do. Maryann wanted to get his license number. Then the police could run the plate. That would certainly be helpful.

"Maryann, can we set up the sprinkler? Bobby and I want to run through it. It's hot out here."

She turned to Aaron. "Oh, of course, we can. But I want to set it up in the back, not out here in the front yard. Can you get the sprinkler yourself?"

Aaron shook his head solemnly. "Mommy says I can't go into the shed alone because there's too many things there that could hurt me."

"Your mother's right. I'll be right with you." Her mind, momentarily distracted, returned to thoughts of the watcher. But as she started to walk up the street toward the Mercedes, the car took off making an abrupt U-turn and going in the opposite direction, burning rubber. Maryann stood there in frustration, hands on hips for a few moments. She really had a bad feeling about this.

Jen placed her purchases in the picnic cooler she kept in the trunk of the car. Her produce would stay crisp and fresh until she returned to the house. In the meantime, she intended to browse around Main Street for a few extra minutes. She chose the bakery as her first stop. She had a yen for chocolate cake. Maybe it had been caused by talking to Grant Coleman a few minutes ago. She had to admit that seeing him depressed her. They had no relationship, never had one, and yet she still felt as if they should have. For those few glorious weeks when they worked together on the Shakespeare project, she'd been so happy. But that joy had been totally crushed. Being reminded of the pain made her miserable. Yes, she would prescribe chocolate cake for this evening. It might not serve as a cure for depression, but it wouldn't hurt either. A good thing she wasn't overweight.

Before walking into Bigelow's Bakery, Jen again noticed the shop between the bakery and the bookstore that stood vacant. She became thoughtful. A coffee shop at that location did seem like a good idea. People could buy a treat at the bakery and take it into the coffee shop to sit down and relax, perhaps socialize. Others might purchase a book or magazine and want to do the same. Maryann's idea of offering lattes and cappuccinos wasn't half-bad.

They wouldn't really be competing with the diner because that establishment served regular coffee, usually with breakfast, lunch or dinner. The cash her grandmother had so generously made available to her could pay the rent on the shop and serve to renovate it. But she had no knowledge or ability in the area of business. Jen knew her limitations. Her work life had been spent in a laboratory. She'd never related well to other people, too shy, too reserved. It was only with Bill that she'd felt comfortable enough to reach out. Again she thought how fortunate she'd been to have him in her life and also to have given birth to his son.

If only Maryann could remain in Bloomingvale. Perhaps then she could manage the courage to create a business and a new life for herself and Aaron. Maybe in time she would be able to make plans. She stared at the empty shop and sighed.

Jen visited Bigelow's Bakery and eyed the different cakes in the display case.

Mrs. Bigelow came over to wait on her.

"Can I have the chocolate cake with the shavings on top?"

"Sure thing. It's double chocolate, got chocolate chips inside as well. I'll just put that in a box for you."

"Look who's buying cake to eat while her own mother is starving."

Jen turned around startled. "Are you really starving?"

Sara Morrow turned a sour look on her daughter. "Would you really care if I were?"

"Yes, I can certainly spare some money."

"How much?" An index finger with a long blood-red fingernail pointed at her. "I want a million dollars. Give it to me and I'll drop my lawsuit."

Jen shook her head. "You know I don't have that kind of money. Two years from now I might."

The accusing finger aimed at her like a weapon. "Two years? A lot can happen in two years. I could be dead in two years, or you could be."

Her mother turned and stormed out of the bakery. Jen watched her leave and realized she'd been holding her breath. Mrs. Bigelow, who'd been staring, now held the boxed cake out to her. Jen's face flushed with embarrassment. Her hands shook.

As she drove back to the house, she realized that never once had her mother inquired about her grandson. Apparently, she cared only about money. It made Jen sick to her stomach.

When she arrived home, it looked as if Maryann had been waiting for her. Her friend wore an odd expression.

"I'm sorry. Did I take too long?"

Maryann ripped at a fingernail. "It's not that. I thought you should know about something."

"Are the boys all right?" She felt a sense of alarm from the way Maryann behaved.

"No, nothing like that. They're both fine. In fact, Aaron wants to know if Bobby can stay for dinner. They're in his room now playing soldiers."

"Then what is it?" She knew something was troubling her friend.

"Probably nothing. But there happened to be a man in a car sitting up the street. I got the impression he was watching us."

"You mean you and the boys?"

Maryann gave a quick nod. "Yes. When I started to go toward the car, he turned and drove away."

"Did you see his face?"

Maryann frowned. "I couldn't. He slouched down in the car. Come to think about it, he wore a baseball hat with the bill pulled low."

Jen absently placed the groceries on the marble tile flooring in the foyer. "I have to say what you're telling me makes me feel very uneasy."

"I know. Think we should call Chief Coleman?"

The thought of seeing him again today made her feel ill. What would he think? Probably that she was chasing after him, making up stories to get his attention. Of course, it was Maryann's narrative not her own. Still, she felt he would be suspicious.

"Maybe we ought to wait and see. Besides, what can we tell Grant Coleman? Can you describe the man?"

Maryann shook her head.

"Did you get a license plate?"

"No, I tried but he left too fast. I did see the car. It happened to be a silver Mercedes, a recent model from what I could tell."

"Well, frankly, it doesn't have to mean anything at all. Maybe he just saw a beautiful woman and wanted to ogle you."

"Thanks for the compliment. I suppose you could be right. It doesn't have to be the same person or persons that have been harassing us."

"You mean me. And no, it doesn't. I think I've been bothering Chief Coleman too much. We'll give him a pass on this incident. I doubt there's any need to worry."

"All right, if you say so. What did you buy for dinner?"

"Good stuff."

Maryann picked up the bakery box. "What about this?"

Jen smiled and shrugged. "I think the boys are entitled to a little treat, and so are we. It's a chocolate chip chocolate cake."

"My day just improved."

"Mine too. Want to help me fix dinner?"

"Of course," Maryann said, picking up the package of groceries. "What are friends for?"

Chapter Forty-Two

Jen perspired profusely while working in the kitchen. The window air conditioner would need some adjustment. She and Maryann had fixed chicken salad, potato salad, cole slaw and various nibbles for their picnic basket. They'd squeezed fresh lemons for their lemonade as well.

"I understand a church group sells hot dogs and hamburgers as a fund raiser. You know Aaron will prefer that."

"No question," Maryann agreed.

"They'll also have ice cream and ices there. So I don't think we want to take anymore with us."

"I think you're right." Maryann wiped the sweat from her own brow. "This should hold us."

"I'll try and make myself and Aaron scarce for a while so you and Rob can have some alone time."

Maryann shrugged and trained her eyes on the floor. "It really isn't necessary."

"I kind of think it is. You do like him, don't you?"

"Sure. He's a terrific guy. But you know I'm leaving. I don't think he accepts that."

Jen didn't comment. This was Maryann's business. She didn't want to offer an unwanted opinion or any advice. Maryann as a mature woman obviously knew her own mind. And yet a real relationship, one in which both parties truly connected wasn't easy to find. Jen had a strong feeling that Rob and Maryann could make a go of it together.

The doorbell rang and Aaron called out that he would answer it. Jen suspected her son knew that Rob would be arriving at any minute and had been waiting for him. Rob endured as one of Aaron's favorite people. She liked that arrangement. Rob had not become a father substitute but more like an uncle.

"Rob's here," Aaron announced, which proved unnecessary since the man in question followed her son out to the kitchen.

"Let me put those hampers in your car for you," Rob said.

"We're not quite ready yet," Jen told him.

"When you are, let me know. I just did the same thing for my mother and sisters."

"How are they?"

Rob moved his head from side to side. "Fine. Bringing lots of food too."

"Come to my room." Aaron took Rob's large hand with his small one and pulled him along. "I built this humongous skyscraper and put King Kong on top. Wait 'til you see it."

"Well, I can't miss that." Rob flashed a broad grin at Aaron and then turned back to Jen and Maryann. "Call me when you're ready to go."

Jen waited until Rob left the kitchen with Aaron. Then she turned back to Maryann. "That man will be a good father someday."

"I suppose so." Maryann's eyes did not meet hers and so it was impossible to know what her friend might be thinking. "I think I'll go upstairs and change."

"I guess I should do the same, get out of these messy clothes."

As they ascended the stairs, Jen heard the sound of childish laughter and Rob's deep mellifluous voice. She smiled to herself. This would be a memorable day. She felt it in her bones.

The watcher lurked, waiting to see if the two women and the child happened to be alone. He observed the big man with the strong muscled build drive up to the house in a pick-up truck and felt dismay. He'd seen this man before working on the house. But today wasn't a work day. He'd parked too close last time and nearly been spotted. Too close for comfort. He couldn't afford that. Surveillance cameras had been set up at the house so he dared not risk any further acts of vandalism.

He would be seen. He would be caught. He would be sent to jail. That couldn't happen. It was unthinkable.

Acts of vandalism hadn't worked. Other means would have to be used. He had an inventive mind, a fine level of creativity. He had tried to drive the Stoddard woman from the house, deemed it imperative. But she'd proven stubborn.

His mind energized with different ideas. He must get rid of the woman, and the sooner the better. Today he needed to do something radical. She'd forced him to it with her obtuse stupidity. Her own fault. Not his. She made this necessary. He watched from his vantage as the muscle man placed food baskets in the back of a pick-up truck. So the man would be driving them. That was unfortunate. He had thought of forcing them off the road. But that would be best done when they were out on the highway. He might use his rifle again if necessary. He felt prepared. He'd even purchased several handguns on the streets of Kansas City the last time he visited, ones that could not be traced. He envisioned himself forcing the Stoddard woman off the road and shooting her dead in the dark of night on a deserted road. He smiled at the pleasing thought.

He'd worked on the brakes of that rental car. But she'd been with the other woman at the time. He hadn't wanted to kill them both. However, he felt desperate enough to do that now.

Things had changed. He'd watch and wait for the right opportunity to eliminate her. He could be flexible. Her fault, all of it, her fault.

He'd almost killed her back when she arrived. Shooting at her through the open window of the car hadn't been a bad idea. Of course, he'd only meant to frighten her into leaving then. But if she had been killed, so much the better. It seemed totally justified.

She'd had enough warnings. Today matters would need to take a more serious turn. He'd up the ante. He only had to wait and watch. All her fault! She would have to pay the price in blood.

Chapter Forty-Three

Jen was having a nice time at the Labor Day picnic, mostly because Aaron was enjoying himself. Seeing her son happy made her happy as well.

"How are you doing?"

Jen looked up from her cleaning. "Keeping the ants off the blanket as best I can."

Linda Coleman laughed. "Good luck with that." Jen observed that Linda looked cheerful and years younger than her age. Hard work must agree with her. But Jen had noticed that Linda maintained a positive attitude toward life very different from her own mother.

"Where are Lori and Sue?"

"Trying to flirt with the musicians. Those young men are about their age. Myself, I can't stand that loud music. I guess I'm showing my age."

"I'm not crazy about it either," Jen said.

"I brought you one of my homemade apple pies for dessert." She set the covered dish down on the picnic blanket.

"We've been hearing a lot about your pies." Maryann smiled at Linda.

"Probably from Rob. He's the pie lover in the family."

"You'll have to teach me how to bake them," Jen said.

"It would be my pleasure."

"Why don't we leave the pie with you for now though? We can join you later at your picnic table. I'm afraid if we leave it here, the ants will be feasting instead of us." Jen handed the pie plate back to Linda.

"Are they having fireworks?" Maryann asked.

"No, that's only on the fourth of July. It's the bigger summer holiday here. The town does a picnic on Memorial Day as well but it's more like this one. See you all later."

Jen looked around and saw more familiar faces. Dr. Kramer, his wife and daughter were present and chatting with Noah Winthrop, the local dentist. Dave Stuart, the mechanic who worked on her car, flirted with Terrie Prentice, the young woman who worked at the bookstore.

"Having a good time, Mrs. Stoddard?" Jen turned to see Samuel Forrest.

He hadn't dressed formally in suit and tie as she'd seen him last, but even his casual clothes spoke of quality. His slacks were perfectly creased.

"How are you, Mr. Forrest?"

"I would be doing better if you hadn't sent that policeman around to bother me."

"I did not send him."

He gave her a look that indicated he didn't believe her one bit. "You may come to regret your actions."

Jen stiffened. "Are you threatening me?"

"Not at all. But there is an old saying: what comes around goes around. I'm certain you're familiar with that. Good day, Mrs. Stoddard." His eyes reminded her of granite.

Jen shivered slightly as Samuel Forrest made his way through the convivial crowd.

"What a creepy little man," Maryann observed. "I guess there are nasty people everywhere, even in friendly small towns like this one."

When it was time to join the Higgins family, they gathered together the remains of their picnic lunch, discarded the perishable leftovers, and for the moment left everything else behind.

Eric Higgins had a grill going and continued to barbecue. "Bobby and I were coming to get you. We still have some time before the relay race begins. Thought you might like some of this."

"How thoughtful," Jen said.

"Got lots of food here." Eric pointed with a spatula. Choice of hamburgers, cheeseburgers, grilled chicken, sausage and peppers, corn on the cob, baked beans, cole slaw, pasta salad, and potato salad, cookies, and soda. Help yourselves."

"No thanks," Aaron said. "If I eat anymore I won't be able to run."

"Well, I'm not running," Rob said. He helped himself to a cheeseburger and took a large bite. "I like the way you cooked this." He turned to Eric. "Usually burgers are burned on the outside when they're grilled."

Eric flashed a big smile. "The secret is waiting until the coals turn white and glow. Then you put the meat on and get perfect even cooking. Gotta have patience though."

Rob nodded. "Yeah, patience is the key to getting lots of things right." He glanced over at Maryann and gave her a meaningful look.

They remained with the Higgins family during the relay race, the hundred-yard dash and the three-legged race. Jen cheered for the boys, but they were disheartened because they lost all three races.

"There's always next year, sport," Rob said, mussing Aaron's hair.

"We'll probably be in New York," Aaron muttered, his eyes cast down.

Jen felt a sense of alarm. Aaron still believed they were going back to the city, that this had been only a vacation. She would have to talk to him, explain things, make it clear once and for all that they would be living in Bloomingvale permanently, at least for the next two years. Aaron would have to come to terms with her decision. But would he able to accept it as she hoped?

Chapter Forty-Five

Rob turned to Maryann. "Would you take a walk with me?"

She looked up at him. "Just the two of us?"

"If you don't mind."

"See you later," Jen said.

"Where should we look for you?"

"I'll be right here with the Higgins family. Aaron wants to remain with Bobby.

I think there will be other children too that Bobby will introduce to Aaron."

"Sounds like a plan," Rob said. "We'll see you in a little while."

He took Maryann's hand in his own larger one and glanced over at her as they strolled along."

After they walked along Main Street for a block, Maryann stopped and turned to him. "Why did you want to be alone with me?"

"Well, for starters, I need to walk off some of that good food."

"But you have another reason, don't you?"

"I do." He gazed into her eyes. "I wish I was a romantic kind of guy. I'm sure in New York men bring you flowers and champagne, send limousines for you. Best I could manage is a bouquet of wild flowers, some local wine and a ride in my pick-up truck."

She smiled. "I'm not as fussy as you think."

"Good to know." He smiled back at her. He took her hand to his mouth and kissed each finger in turn, then turned her hand over and kissed the palm. She emitted a deep sigh which he took as his reward.

He swallowed hard.

"I guess I haven't made it a secret how I feel about you. I know you haven't wanted to get too involved with me."

She looked up at him, shading her eyes from the sun with her hands. "I just don't want to hurt you or myself. You know I'm leaving here in a couple of days. I have a whole life back in New York. We've discussed this before. I don't think there's anything left to say."

Rob felt his heart begin to hammer. "That's where you're wrong. There's plenty to say. I just don't know if I can say it right. I'll just come out with it, no fancy language. I love you. I loved you from the first moment I laid eyes on you."

Maryann pulled her hand from his and shook her head vehemently, her hair moving like a wheat field in the wind. "I don't believe in that love at first sight stuff. You can be attracted to someone physically, of course, but you can't love them. Rob, we still hardly know each other. How can you say you love me? It's so unrealistic."

"I do know you though. We've talked. We've spent time together. Okay, I admit, there is a strong physical attraction, at least for me. But it's so much more than that. I'm a man. I know my own mind and my own heart. I want to ask you to marry me. I want to buy you a ring. I want to build you a house just the way you want it built. I want to live in that house with you and raise children with you. I want us to have a life together."

Maryann increased her pace as if to put distance between them. He pulled her around and found that she was crying. Tears streamed down her flushed cheeks.

"I'm not a domestic person like your mother and sisters. I won't just sit in a house day after day. I need to work."

"My mother started her own business. Why can't you start a business here?"

"Do they really need another sweet shop in town?"

"Honey, a smart woman like you can figure out something to do. You can build your own business."

She shook her head in denial. "I can't see Bloomingvale as a place for opportunities."

"Maybe not for earning millions, but do you really need a fortune to be happy? Isn't there more to life than getting rich?

Let me tell you something, money won't keep you warm in bed on a cold winter's night. Money can't love you the way I will." Rob took Maryann in his arms and kissed her with all the passion and love he felt for her. For a moment, she kissed him back with equal intensity.

"You do love me too, don't you? Sweetheart, take the risk and marry me. All of life is a gamble. You know that don't you? No one knows what's going to happen tomorrow. It could be good. It could be terrible. But we have this time together. We have right now and we should seize the moment. Marry me, darling. I promise you won't regret it."

For a moment, she stared at him, eyes jungle green and unblinking. "You can't guarantee that. No, I can't marry you. Don't ask me again." She began to run away down the street.

"Where are you going?"?

"I'm going back to the house."

"I'll get the truck and drive you."

"No, I want to walk. I need a long walk. Just tell Jen and Aaron. I'll see them later." With that, she took off.

Rob stuck his fists into the pockets of his jeans and slowly walked back toward the picnic. For a moment, he'd been certain that she loved him too. Then she'd rejected him.

He stalked off looking for where he'd left Jen Stoddard and Aaron.

He found them right where they'd been before with the Higgins family. Jennifer and Maggie were talking together. Aaron was playing with Bobby Higgins and some other children. Nothing had changed for them. Everything had changed for him. In spite of what his mother said or believed, he knew he'd never love another woman the way he loved Maryann. It couldn't happen.

Jen noticed him and glanced around. "Where's Maryann?"

"She decided to walk back to the house. She didn't want me to drive her. I'm planning on leaving myself."

"Right now?" Jen Stoddard looked surprised.

"Yes, as a matter of fact. Do you want to pack up? I'll drive you back to your house."

Jen looked over at her son. "Aaron's having such a good time right now, I'd hate to make him leave."

Maggie took Jen's arm. "We have room in the S.U.V. for you." Maggie turned to him. "Eric and I will drive Jen and Aaron home later."

Jen gave Rob a speculative look. "Rob, are you all right?"

He didn't answer. He couldn't. He stuck his fisted hands back into his pockets and hurried away.

Chapter Forty-Six

Jen had an odd sense of being watched. She looked around. No one seemed to be looking in her direction. She tried to shake the feeling. Was Samuel Forrest still lurking about? If so, that might explain her strange feeling.

Jen heard some shouting and looked over at the boys. They were playing soccer. Bobby served as goalie. Aaron barreled into him trying to score. They both tumbled and fell. Bobby shouted his indignation and punched Aaron in the face. Aaron retaliated by kicking Bobby. Jen started toward them with Maggie following.

"Let them settle it themselves," Eric called after them. "Don't get involved."

But Jen ran to separate the two boys. Maggie pulled Bobby back.

"Apologize," Maggie said to her son.

Bobby shook his head, a lock of hair falling into his face. "No, he started it."

"You were both wrong," Jen said. "You should apologize to each other and shake hands."

The boys weren't having it.

"My nose is bleeding," Aaron told her.

"Okay, let's go back to our picnic blanket. I have ice in the chest."

"I don't like Bobby anymore." Aaron said, holding his nose.

"You'll be good friends again. Even friends have arguments sometimes."

Aaron shook his head. "Can we leave here with Rob and Maryann? I want to go home. I don't want to stay here anymore."

Jen had a sinking feeling. "Honey, let me make an ice pack for your nose. You'll feel much better then."

Aaron kicked a soda can that lay on the grass. "Wanna go home."

"Honey, we'll go back to the house soon."

"No, wanna go home to New York."

She found the ice in the chest, wrapped a cloth around it and made an ice pack for Aaron. "Hold this against your nose and it will feel better soon. The bleeding's already stopped." She kept her tone of voice soothing. But Aaron continued to be upset. His face had flushed scarlet. Jen recognized he'd become overheated and overtired. The day had been too much for him.

"I want to go home to New York," he repeated again, this time more adamantly.

Jen felt herself losing her patience with her son. "Honey, we are going to live in Bloomingvale for the next two years. You know that. You'll go to school here and I believe you'll be happy."

"No!" Aaron threw the ice pack down.

As Jen bent to retrieve it, he took off running. "Aaron!" she called after him, but her son was losing himself in the throng of people. Jen started after him, keeping her eyes on the receding back of her son, only to fall hard. A child had left a skateboard out. She skinned her knee and her hands burned, but she made an effort to get back in motion again.

"Are you all right?" A man spoke to her solicitously. "Here let me help you up."

"I'm looking for my son. He's running ahead of me."

"Yes, I saw him. A red-headed boy I believe?"

"How did you know?"

"We've met. Don't you remember?"

Jen took a closer look. "Mr. Norris. You're James Donne's nephew, the accountant."

The man smiled at her. "The very same. I saw you earlier with your son. I suppose you didn't see me."

"I'm sorry, I didn't."

"There are a great many people here today. Actually, I had every intention of speaking to you, but you've been surrounded by people all afternoon."

"Forgive me, but right now, I must find my son. So if you'll excuse me."

He took her arm and held on to it with a firm grasp. "I intend to help you look for him. As a matter of fact, I know exactly where he went. Another man stopped him and they went toward his car."

Alarm bells sounded in Jen's mind. "What man? Do you know who he is?"

"I can't be certain. Why don't we look together?"

"Yes, please show me."

"Of course. We'll hurry."

Jen felt close to panic. Had someone abducted Aaron? Would he even go with a stranger? She thought of her mother's boyfriend, then of Samuel Forrest. Would either of them go so far as to attempt to kidnap her son? She couldn't believe it possible!

Edward Norris seemed stronger than he looked. A man in his middle to late forties, he was lean and athletic. He moved quickly, practically dragging her along at his pace. Jen soon had trouble catching her breath in the humid air. Norris led her along a path that appeared devoid of people, a deserted area. She did see a car in the distance, a silver Mercedes. Was it the vehicle Maryann had described to her? She broke away from Norris and began to run toward the car. She called out her son's name.

But as she came closer to the car, Jen could see there was no one in it. Where was the man Mr. Norris spoke of? More importantly, where was Aaron? Norris took her arm again, practically clamping down on it.

"Where are they?" she said. "Where can they be?"

"Let's look back here." He guided her toward the back of the car.

The trunk opened. Suddenly Edward Norris tried to push her into it. Jen cried out in surprise and shock. It took all her strength to keep her balance and avoid being forced into the car's trunk.

"What are you doing?"

"Get into the trunk." Norris removed a small automatic weapon from his pants pocket and pointed it at her.

Jen stared at the weapon. Sunlight pirouetted off the black gun barrel. "What are you doing? Where is my son?"

"I have no idea. I doubt that anyone's snatched him if that makes you feel any better."

Jen realized she had been targeted. "You're the one, aren't you? All along you've been trying to harass and harm me. But why? We don't even know each other."

"Can't you guess? No, I suppose not. But you would have found out eventually. You were too curious about the money. You would have insisted on a full accounting. And then you would have discovered the million-dollar short fall."

Jen shook her head in disbelief. "You stole my grandmother's money?"

"I borrowed. I didn't steal. It just didn't work out. Damn bad economy. I couldn't pay the money back. And now, into the trunk of the car, my dear."

"No, I refuse." Jen knew she would be dead for certain if she did as he told her.

"Then I will just have to shoot you here. Either way, you will be dead. Get in the trunk."

He waved the gun with a menacing gesture.

Jen's mind worked with frantic speed. Would he really shoot her here? There were people not that far away. Surely someone would hear gunshots. But would they be in time to save her? She couldn't take that risk, could she? She had to outsmart him.

"All right," she said. "I'll get into the trunk."

Jen turned as if to comply with his dictates, then ran toward a clump of trees instead.

She heard a bullet whiz by but kept on moving, her heart in her mouth. She felt something sting her left arm.

Chapter Forty-Seven

Grant observed Aaron Stoddard running, his nose bloody, his shirt torn. The boy had tears rolling down his cheeks. Something was very wrong. Where was Jennifer Stoddard?

He chased the boy down and stopped him. "Where you headed, son?"

"I'm running away!" The child responded to him in a breathless voice.

"Let's get you a drink of water. Your face is red. Where's your mother?"

"I don't know. I left her. She said we can't go back to New York. We have to live here. I don't want to live here. I want to go home. I have my school in New York. My friends are there."

"Well, you'll have to work that out with her. But she must be frantic worrying about you right now. Let's go find her."

"She's probably with Mrs. Higgins."

They walked to where the Higgins family was located.

"Have you seen Aaron's mother?" Grant asked.

"I just saw Jen walking off in that direction with that accountant." Maggie pointed. She then turned to her husband. "Eric, what's the name of the accountant who did our taxes?"

"That would be Ed Norris."

"What was she doing with him?" Grant wondered out loud.

Maggie shook her head. "I don't know. He had his hand on her arm like he intended to take her somewhere or show her something."

"Keep Aaron with you."

"Sure, we were going to take Jen and Aaron home."

Grant ran in the direction Maggie had indicated. He had an uncomfortable feeling that something wasn't right. His cop instinct told him that Jennifer Stoddard wouldn't be walking off with Norris when she had every reason to worry about her child.

He heard the unmistakable sound of shots ringing out and unsnapped his holstered weapon as he ran. He saw Norton not far from a car with a gun drawn. Was he intending to shoot Jennifer Stoddard? Grant had the gut instinct that was the case.

"Drop your weapon!" he shouted, raising his own gun.

The accountant turned around, his eyes wild and pointed the handgun at him.

"If you don't drop your weapon and put your hands behind your head this instant, I'm going to have to shoot you. Do you understand?"

Norton did as he was told. Grant cuffed him, hands behind his back and forced the man face down on the ground. He kept his foot on the small of Norton's back as he used his cell phone to call for back-up.

"Okay, now where's Mrs. Stoddard?" When Norton didn't answer immediately, Grant readied himself to give the man a hard kick. Then he heard the cry for help. He left Norton, warning him to stay where he was and not move.

He found Jennifer Stoddard, lying on the ground at some distance from Norton almost covered by dead leaves. Her arm had bled out from a bullet hole. He immediately took a clean handkerchief from his pocket and pressed it against the wound.

"Thank you for finding me," she said, her voice barely audible. "He wanted to kill me." She explained about the embezzlement of funds from her grandmother's account. Then she fainted in his arms.

He used his cell phone again and called for an ambulance. Burt Russell soon arrived and took charge of Edward Norris. Grant told him to read Norris his rights and hold him in custody.

He rode with Jennifer Stoddard to the hospital in the ambulance, holding her hand, after reassuring her that her son was fine. He did his best to comfort her, kissing her forehead, caressing her cheek. He realized that he wasn't behaving in a professional manner, that his feelings for her went a lot deeper than he cared to admit but somehow he couldn't help it.

As he waited in the hospital corridor, Grant phoned Maryann Waller and told her what had happened. She in turn told him about seeing the silver Mercedes previously.

"You should have told me at the time," he said.

"Jen asked me not to bother you."

"You shouldn't have listened to her."

"I'm sorry." He had reprimanded her and hoped it hadn't come off as too harsh, but Jennifer could have easily been dead.

"Will Jen be all right?"

"They're treating her right now. She was lucky Norris isn't much of a marksman. It could have gone the other way."

"What should I tell Aaron?"

"Just that his mother had an accident. She's okay and will come home soon. Maggie and Eric Higgins are going to bring Aaron home."

"Yes, in fact, they just pulled into the driveway."

"Okay. Don't worry. Your friend really is going to be fine."

Grant checked on Jennifer after the doctor told him it was all right to see her. She looked as pale as the sheets.

"How are you feeling?"

She managed a wry smile. "I've felt better. But I'm alive and grateful to you for that."

"Actually, I think you saved yourself with your own fast thinking. Norris must have derailed."

"He did steal a great deal of money. He says he lost it gambling."

"They going to take the bullet out soon?" He stared at her bandaged arm.

She moved her head from side to side. "The bullet only grazed my arm. They're giving me antibiotics as a precaution against infection, but I'm all right."

He took her hand in his and sat down beside her. "You gave me a scare," he said.

"How did you know what happened or where to even look for me?"

"Cop radar."

She gave him a dubious look and he laughed. "Okay, I'll confess. I saw your kid running and crying. So I knew something had to be wrong. When I asked him where you were, he told me about the argument you guys had. He thought you might have gone back to the Higgins family. When I asked Maggie, she told me she'd seen you walking with Norris. That sounded off. So I took myself in the general direction she'd seen you go and I heard the gunshots."

"At least I had the presence of mind not to get into the trunk of his car. He tried to force me but I got away from him. Thank you for saving me, for rescuing me. Thank you for helping my son as well."

"Just doing my job, Ma'am."

"And you do it very well indeed."

He caressed her cheek. She held his hand tightly in her own. "I always knew you were a hero."

He pulled away. "I don't know why you'd say that."

"Because it's true. I forgave you for what you did to me back in high school. I suppose you don't even remember."

"What I did to you?" He felt incredulous.

He heard her call after him in an alarmed voice as he left, but he didn't turn around. He'd had enough.

Chapter Forty-Eight

Maryann felt relieved when she found out that Jen would be released from the hospital the following day. She took Aaron with her to pick up Jen at the hospital. Aaron rushed into his mother's arms.

"I'm sorry. I shouldn't have run away like that. I should have been there to protect you from that bad man."

Jen hugged her son with her good arm. "It wasn't your fault."

"Maryann says I should give Bloomingvale a chance, that's it's a good place to live."

Maryann patted his head. "That's right. I think you'll like going to school here. You'll have an adjustment to make, but it's going to be fine."

Jen turned to her. "Thank you." There were tears in her eyes.

"How's the arm?"

"Could have been a whole lot worse."

Maryann spoke to Aaron. "Honey, can you wait in the hall while I help your mom get dressed so she can be discharged?"

"Sure."

Jen frowned at him. "Don't go exploring. Stay right outside this room in the hallway." Jen turned to her after he left. "He can be too curious."

"So I've noticed." Maryann pulled the curtain around for privacy. "I brought a change of clothes for you. Do you need some help?"

"I think I might."

As she helped Jen change, Maryann thought that her friend appeared fatigued. There were shadows beneath her eyes. "Did you get any rest here?"

"For a little while, but hospitals have lots of noise even in the middle of the night. Nurses and aides are constantly coming in and out. I just want to get back to the house."

"I can't believe that man actually tried to kill you."

"I'd rather not talk about it right now. I haven't come to terms with it yet. Let's discuss something else. What went on between you and Rob Coleman?"

Maryann bit her lower lip. "He asked me to marry him. He said that he loved me."

Jen took her hands. "Oh, how wonderful! But why do you look so unhappy?"

Maryann lowered her eyes. "I told him I couldn't accept."

"I'm so sorry. You don't love him?"

Maryann shrugged uneasily. "It's not that simple. I have a life in New York. He would expect me to give up everything and come here to live. How can I do that?"

Jen's look expressed sympathy. "Sometimes, a person needs time to think things out before making a decision, especially a life-altering one like this. You could explain that to him."

Maryann ran her hands through her hair. "I don't think so."

"Can I ask you a blunt question?" Jen met her gaze with a direct look.

"Of course, ask away."

"Do you love Rob?"

"It's complicated."

"Not if you really love the man. You can work this out together."

She helped Jen into her shirt and then her shorts, thinking hard. "His home, family and business are all in Bloomingvale. I don't have a life here except as a visitor."

"I believe you could make a life here if you wanted it enough. Nothing is ever going to be perfect. But with some ingenuity, you could make it work. Nothing stays the same. With the right person, life can be satisfying and meaningful."

Maryann smiled at her friend. "Jen you are such an optimist and a romantic."

"I do believe in love," Jen said.

179

"You have given me something to think about," she admitted. "But it's probably too late for Rob and me. I did refuse him. I think he's an all or nothing kind of guy."

Jen shrugged. "Maybe not. I have a feeling he's not a man who gives up easily."

Jen felt much more like herself the following day. Maryann fixed breakfast for them then drove her and Aaron to the elementary school. Since he was a new student, a lot of paperwork had to be filled out. Jen felt glad that Aaron's behavior had settled down.

Jen had nearly forgotten that Linda Coleman and her daughters were scheduled to clean the house later that morning. Maryann helped her straighten up a bit, putting things away so there wouldn't be a mess.

Linda Coleman arrived looking cheerful and carrying a pie.

"You didn't have to do that," Jen said, touched by Linda's thoughtfulness.

"Well, you never did get to taste my pie at the Labor Day picnic, so I thought I'd bake a fresh one to welcome you back from the hospital."

"I wasn't there very long, only overnight."

"Just the same, there's nothing like a sweet treat to make a body feel better."

"Why don't we all sit down together later and have the pie? Maryann and I will put up a pot of coffee."

Linda looked pleased. Her daughters came into the foyer. They carried their equipment and cleaning supplies. Linda spoke to Lori and Sue. "Let's get started." She turned back to Jen. "We'll look forward to sitting down with you after we finish."

Jen went out in the backyard and pulled a chaise into the shade. She didn't want to oversee the cleaning operation. It seemed important that Linda Coleman understood she was trusted. As for Maryann, her friend went upstairs to start packing her things for the trip back to New York.

Jen must have dozed off because the next thing she knew, Linda spoke to her. "All done for today," she said.

Jen got to her feet, still a little bleary. "I'll get my wallet."

"No rush. Why don't we have the pie first?"

Jen followed Linda back through the side door of the house, up the stairs into the large, old-fashioned kitchen. Lori and Sue waited on their mother.

"I'll have the coffee ready in a few minutes, or would you prefer tea?" Jen looked from Linda to each of her daughters.

The young women exchanged looks. "Actually we have to go. We have another job waiting for us." Lori fixed her eyes on the floor.

"You go ahead," Linda said.

"If we take the truck, how will you get there?" Sue knit her brows.

"I'll take your mom over," Jen said.

"Go on," Linda urged her daughters. "I'll be along soon."

The young women didn't look happy about it, but they did as their mother told them and left.

"I'm sorry," Jen said. "I didn't mean to make them uncomfortable."

Linda shrugged. "We don't normally socialize with people we work for. It's kind of an unwritten rule."

"I don't feel as if you work for me," Jen said. "You help me."

Linda smiled. "But you pay us. That's the difference."

"On the other hand, you didn't have to bake me a pie."

The tea kettle soon whistled. "I can offer instant coffee or a few different varieties of tea. I don't brew coffee very often I'm afraid."

"Tea would be fine."

Jen took out green tea bags, put them in cups and poured boiled water over them. "I'll let Maryann know we're ready." She went out to the hall and called upstairs. Sound carried well in the house. Jen appreciated the good acoustics. Maryann soon joined them.

"When are you leaving?" Linda asked.

"Jen's driving me to the airport tomorrow morning."

"Rob will be sorry to see you leave."

Maryann lowered her eyes and dipped her tea bag several times. "I suppose he told you what happened."

"He did."

"I'm really sorry." Maryann looked ready to burst into tears.

"I don't offer opinions. I've made too many mistakes in my own life to have the nerve to tell others what they should or should not do. So I'll not get involved. My son is an adult and so are you. We each have to follow the dictates of our own heart."

Jen decided it might be best to change the subject. "This pie looks wonderful."

"This time I baked a cherry pie. I hope you like it."

"I'm certain we will." Jen began cutting pieces of the pie and placing them into plates.

In the back of her mind she thought of Grant's reaction to her comment that she'd forgiven him. It perplexed her.

Chapter Forty-Nine

Maryann felt out of sync on the cab ride from Kennedy Airport to her apartment on the East side of Manhattan.

She wheeled her suitcases to her bedroom only to find unfamiliar clothing had been strewn over her bed. A scent of stale smoke permeated the room. Someone else's laptop sat on the desk she normally used as well. She'd have a talk with Veronica who she sublet from. She suspected Veronica had seen an opportunity to earn some extra rent money during the time she'd been gone.

Jen planned to tackle the attic again. As yet, she hadn't asked Linda to clean up there. More things needed to be examined. Like Maryann, she found antiques interesting. The old objects in the attic were after all part of her family heritage.

Jen heard a car drive up and looked out the front living room window, moving the drapery back just far enough to see who happened to be coming to visit. The sight of Grant Coleman made her heart beat faster.

She didn't wait for him to ring the doorbell, but flung the door open for him as he reached the porch steps. "Come in."

He gave her a wry smile, removing his hat and sunglasses as he entered the house. "You may not welcome me after you hear what I have to tell you."

Jen straightened. Bad news. She could tell. "What is it?" She led him into the living room and indicated a chair.

"I won't dance around. The prosecutor acted quickly. Norris has been arraigned and then bail was set."

"Bail? How can there be any bail?" Jen suppressed a shudder. "The man tried to kill me."

"We know that. But Norris got himself an outstanding criminal defense attorney, one who's got a lot of juice. He convinced the judge that Norris is a model citizen, well-established in the community with family roots here and no priors. So the judge allowed bail to be set. The amount happened to be large, but Norris made it."

She started to feel dizzy. Grant moved fast, taking her into his arms. "Steady."

"I'm all right. I just don't believe it. Are you saying he's free again and he could get off?"

"Unless Norris pleads guilty, and that doesn't seem to be his intention, there will be a trial. You'll testify. I'll testify. We'll put him away for a long time." Grant's words were comforting, reassuring, but she wasn't convinced that would be the case.

"What about all the money he stole?" Jen moved away from Grant and sat down heavily on a sofa, the overstuffed brown velvet one.

"I think the prosecutor's office is looking for restitution."

"Mr. Norris told me he lost a good amount of my grandmother's money."

"Turns out he may have embezzled from more than just your grandmother's account. We're still looking into that." Grant sat down beside her. "Norris still has lots of assets, fancy house, expensive cars, paintings worth a fortune. Looks like he's been stealing from a lot of estate accounts for many years. The more restitution, the shorter his sentence will be. That's if his lawyer chooses to cop a plea."

Jen wrinkled her nose in disgust. "Do you think he'll come after me again?"

"He'd be crazy to do that. We've arranged for an order of protection against him. That way if he comes anywhere near you, he'll be right back in jail again."

A sense of relief washed over her. "Good."

Rob visited the Pritchard house not knowing the reason why Jennifer Stoddard had called him. She hadn't explained on the phone, just asked if he could come over sometime during the day. From the tense tone of her voice, he sensed that the matter was an important one. Rob told her he could make it by sometime after five p.m. She readily agreed.

Now as he rang her doorbell, Rob wondered if this had anything to do with Maryann.

Somehow he doubted it. He couldn't seem to stop thinking about her, wondering if she thought about him as well. But he'd survive. He would hang tough. Hadn't he survived nearly dying while serving his country? People didn't die of broken hearts. That happened only in movies and novels. If only he could turn off his feelings.

He rang the doorbell for the second time and Aaron answered. The boy pulled him into the house.

"My mom said you'd come to see us. Can you stay and have dinner with us?"

Rob didn't know what to say. "We'll see." Being noncommittal seemed best. This appeared to be Aaron's idea, not his mother's. "So where's your mom?"

"Out in the kitchen. She's fixing burgers, turkey ones, not the real meat kind," Aaron confided making a face.

"Well, those are real good too and healthy besides."

Aaron skipped his way out to the kitchen. Rob saw that Jennifer Stoddard seemed busy.

"Want me to come back some other time?"

She dabbed some perspiration from her flushed face. "No, not at all. Now is perfect really."

"Can Rob stay for supper?" Aaron asked.

"Of course, there's plenty of food."

"I don't want to intrude on your meal or your time with Aaron."

"You won't be." Her smile beamed warm and friendly. "We'd love the company."

They made small talk for a time. Aaron told him about his teachers and how much he liked them. "Except for the art teacher. She's always fixing my work. I don't think I'm cut out to be an artist," he leaned over to confide.

Rob laughed. "Don't let it bother you. I wasn't either. Never could draw. Now Sue, she's the artistic one in the family. Don't know where she gets it though. None of the rest of us has any such ability."

"Recessive genes," Jennifer Stoddard said.

"If you say so."

Rob had a pleasant dinner with Aaron and his mother. Afterwards, he offered to help her clean up. But she flatly refused. Aaron, eyeing the dishes, asked if he could be excused to do his homework. After Aaron left the room, Rob remained to talk with Jennifer.

"So what's on your mind?"

She bit down on her full lower lip. "Rob I suppose you heard that Edward Norris is out on bail."

"I did and I think it's a shame."

"We agree completely. The thing is I'm kind of uneasy about it. I wondered if you could arrange to install a good burglar alarm system."

"Sure, but they don't come cheap."

"I have the money. I just need help making the arrangements."

"Not a problem," he assured her. "I'll contact several companies. Get estimates and find out when they're free to do the installation."

"As soon as possible, please."

"Sure. I'll give it top priority."

He saw her eyes brighten with unshed tears. He needed to reassure her.

"Don't worry."

She gave him a nod. He could tell she had choked up on her words. He ought to go, but felt the need to talk to her about Maryann.

"Have you heard from her?"

"Only once so far. I expect she's rather busy right now."

Rob pushed the salt shaker around, not looking up. "How did she sound?"

"A little off, I thought. I suppose that's to be expected. She spent more than a month away from the city. She's got to prepare herself for interviews and that's stressful as well."

He almost pushed the salt shaker off the table but caught it just in time. "I don't suppose she happened to talk about me at all?"

"Rob, let me be frank. Maryann did confide in me. She told me that you proposed."

"Then she also told you how she turned me down."

Jennifer gave a reluctant nod. "Yes, she did."

"Do you think she cares about me?"

"Oh, I know she does."

"But not enough to give up her life in New York?"

Jennifer put her hand on his in a gesture of comfort. "Time will tell. I once read a poem back in high school. Our senior English teacher taught British lit. This was a Tudor poem, a sonnet about a man who chases after a doe, only she's elusive and he can't catch her. Finally, as he sits down under a tree to rest, panting and exhausted, the doe comes to him."

"So the lesson or moral I guess is not to chase too hard."

"If it's meant to be, she'll come back here to you. Maryann is strong-willed. She's the kind of person you have to give some space. When Maryann phones, I'll tell her you've been asking after her."

He expressed his appreciation. "Is there anything else I can do for you besides arranging for the burglar alarm system?"

"Yes, as a matter of fact. Get the air conditioning unit in the kitchen working properly."

"You bet. Think I'll go up and say goodnight to Aaron."

"Yes, do that. He'll talk your ear off though."

"I don't mind. He's a good kid."

"We agree on that."

Chapter Fifty

Maryann thought her first interview at an ad agency went well enough. The interviewer reminded her of someone over stimulated by caffeine. He had a wiry body that was constantly in motion.

"Ken Davis." He shook her hand vigorously with his own manicured one. He seemed only a few years older than herself.

"We're looking for someone creative here," he explained. "We're a young agency with new ideas. Our client list is growing. Tell me, what can you bring to the equation?"

Maryann told the man her background. He nodded, seemed pleased, and didn't interrupt her until she finished.

"What makes you want to switch from pharmaceutical marketing to an ad agency job?"

"I'm looking into a number of career options. I wouldn't mind shaking things up a bit, making a change."

Ken Davis nodded his perfectly coiffed head, not one hair moving or out of place.

"You could fit in here, Maryann. The thing is, are you prepared to work ten hour days? Sometimes when we're working on a project for a client, it's weekends as well to make a deadline. It's a cut throat business quite frankly. Are you prepared for that? We expect total dedication. In fact, we demand it."

"I've been doing that right along. I've been completely devoted to my job."

"You sound like the kind of person we're looking for. We'll be in touch."

Maryann left the offices of Gilborne Associates in something of a daze. She had the feeling she'd be offered the job. The real question was: did she want it? In her mind's eyes she could see Rob Coleman offering her his love, asking her to marry him. The man had truly confused her. What did she want? Was it another job in the city or something completely different?

Jen picked up Aaron from school. "Can I go to Bobby's house?"

"Are the two of you friends again?"

"Sure." Her son wrinkled his brow as if the question made no sense whatever.

She marveled at how quickly the boys made up. Friends one minute, enemies the next, then friends again. Such was the nature of childhood, she supposed.

The telephone rang

When she answered, there was a quick hang-up. She saw no caller I.D. listed. Could it be Edward Norris checking to see if she happened to be at home or was she becoming paranoid?

"Who called? Was it Bobby?"

"No, honey, I believe it was a wrong number." Or so she hoped.

After Aaron changed, Jen drove him over to the Higgins home. Maggie welcomed her. Aaron ran to the backyard to join Bobby and Rufus.

"They need to run around for a while," Maggie observed. "Want to come in for a cup of coffee?"

"I'll visit for a while, but I don't need the coffee. My nerves are edgy as it is."

Maggie eyed her with sympathy. "I know what you've been going through. I heard all about it. We were shocked, couldn't understand how Mr. Norris behaved like that."

"I'm still waking up in the middle of the night with nightmares. I've been holding it together for Aaron's sake, but it hasn't been easy."

Maggie led her into the kitchen. "I've got just the thing. Let me fix you a cup of chamomile tea. It's very relaxing."

Jen agreed. Maggie began humming as she worked.

"So how is your friend? Back in New York?"

"She is and I miss her."

"We could spend more time together," Maggie stirred her tea and then poured some milk into it. "Of course, I work part-time. I like earning the extra money."

"Where do you work?"

"You might ask for whom do I work." Maggie smiled.

"Okay, for whom do you work?"

"Take a guess."

It dawned on her. "Eric?"

"Yep, the local vet needs help. I come in every morning after the kids are in school. Sometimes I work until it's time for them to come home. Depends how much help Eric needs. I mostly do the bookkeeping for him. Manage the paperwork. He has several assistants who are good with the animals. That's not my thing though."

"I think it's great that the two of you can work together."

The boys came into the kitchen. Bobby asked her if Aaron could eat dinner at their house. Jen hesitated. She didn't want to have dinner alone, but Aaron seemed excited at the prospect. Maggie assured her that she would bring Aaron home early. How could she refuse?

It occurred to her that there was no need to cook dinner, not for one person. She decided to drive over to The Red Pepper and order a calzone, one stuffed with broccoli and cheese, her favorite. The crowd in the Italian restaurant seemed lively and convivial. Certainly it would be more cheerful eating here than alone back at the house.

"I'll be eating here," she told the man who took her order.

"Sit down with your order number displayed and we'll find you when it's ready."

She found a small table in the rear corner of the restaurant where she felt unobtrusive and seated herself.

"This spot taken?"

Jen looked up. Her heart fluttered. It always seemed to do so when she came into proximity with Grant Coleman.

"You're welcome to it."

"I hope you don't mind. The place is crowded."

"I would like your company," she said. Maybe she shouldn't have said that. She felt embarrassed by her admission.

He pulled the second chair alongside hers. "I like the gunfighter's seat. That way I can watch the room. Lawman's habit I suppose."

"Do you want to trade seats with me?"

"No, as long as I'm not crowding you."

He was but she had no intention of giving him the satisfaction of knowing that. The virile, male scent of him wafted through her nostrils disconcerting her.

"So where's the little guy tonight?"

"Eating dinner with the Higgins family."

A young waitress arrived with Grant's pasta order and her calzone as well. Like the waitresses at the local diner, she gave Grant a long, lingering smile. "Anything to drink?"

"Just water for me," Jen said. The girl didn't even look in her direction.

"I'll have coffee," Grant said.

"Be right back with it." Her smile held promises.

Jen rolled her eyes. Grant noticed. "She's a friend of my sister Lori."

"Lori must have a lot of friends."

"She does as a matter of fact. So does Sue."

"I'm sure." Her tone was dry.

He threw her an amused look.

She took a bite of her calzone, and burned the roof of her mouth.

Fortunately, the waitress arrived with their beverages and she was able to quench the fire.

"Anything else I can get you?" the voice seemed sultry and suggestive.

"We're fine. Thanks." Grant looked back at Jen.

She managed a quick nod.

"Anything I should know about?"

Jen thought of the hang up call earlier. "I received a phone call earlier with no one answering. The I.D. said 'caller unknown'. It probably didn't mean anything though. I mean lots of people dial wrong numbers."

Grant viewed her with a thoughtful expression. "True enough. But if it should happen to become a pattern, you will let me know. Agreed?"

"Of course."

"Incidentally, the attorney general's office is now investigating The Forrest Foundation. It's looking pretty much like Forrest has been running a scam, a fake charity. He preys on wealthy, elderly women in particular. They tend to be easy marks."

"There are so many worthy charities, it's a shame people like him give them a bad name."

"The best thing is always to do your homework, research how much of the money given actually goes to the needy and how much for administrative costs. It can be eye-opening."

They ate in silence for a time. She had to admit that being near Grant Coleman was intoxicating, a heady pleasure. She didn't really blame those waitresses for flirting with him. A pity she couldn't relax and enjoy the experience. When she nearly knocked over her water, he caught her hand and righted the glass. Just that very brief touch seemed to electrify her.

"Thank you. I seem to be clumsy today."

"You're on edge. It's understandable. You've been through a lot lately. You're not even fully healed from being shot."

She lowered her eyes. His kindness was almost her undoing. She began to choke up.

He must have noticed because he took her hand again and held it firmly in his own.

"As you know, we don't have a large police force here. But I'll make certain that morning and evening one of us cruises by your house. We'll keep on the lookout for anyone or anything suspicious."

"I appreciate that."

"Good. Maybe that will ease the tension for you. Call us if something seems wrong."

She gave a nod.

"Promise?"

"Honor bright."
He laughed. She loved his laugh.

Chapter Fifty-One

The city felt oppressively hot and humid today. For some reason she found the press of people and the bustle annoying. In the past, Maryann had just taken it for granted.

She stepped around a homeless man who lay sprawled on the sidewalk. That morning in the crowded subway, a group of street musicians had entered, played some noise, and then passed around a hat. People put money in out of pure embarrassment. She thought about Bloomingvale and had to admit there was something to be said for small town living.

Maryann had another interview today. She felt prepared, psyched for it. She didn't think the ad agency would be quite the right place for her, but this was Big Pharma where she'd worked since graduating from college. William Stoddard had chosen her to intern for him. He'd encouraged her to get her M.B.A. as well. Bill had recommended her for her job in marketing. He'd been more than a great boss. He'd been her mentor. He'd introduced her to Jen who had become her best friend. His death brought Jen and herself even closer together, since they'd shared the terrible loss of such a fine person.

Maryann took her cell phone out of her suit jacket pocket and pressed Jen's number. She felt a sudden need to talk to her friend. There would be a time difference, but she knew Jen was usually an early riser like herself.

Jen answered on the third ring.

"Hope I didn't wake you up."

"Of course not. I'm just fixing breakfast for Aaron. I'm so glad you called. I've been missing you."

"Same here." She swallowed a lump in her throat.

"I don't know if you want to hear this or not, but Rob Coleman's been asking for you. I believe he still cares for you."

She didn't answer. She couldn't seem to find her voice.

"Maryann, are you there?"

"Yes, I'm here. I've got another interview this morning."

"That's good. You'll kill it."

"Maybe. I hope so."

"You'll let me know how it goes?"

"I'll be in touch shortly."

With some effort, she broke the connection.

Jen decided that she would tackle the attic again this morning. This time she would organize everything there. Get rid of the clutter. See what appeared to be of value, sentimental and otherwise. Maryann had been helpful but there was so much else that needed to be examined.

She took her dusting brush and a roll of paper towels with her. No sense bothering Linda to do everything. She felt perfectly capable of handling some of the cleaning herself. Jen picked up a flashlight and took that with her as well. The overhead lights in the attic didn't light up every nook and cranny.

In the attic, she shut the fan and opened one large window. There didn't happen to be a screen on it, but she'd rather endure a few insects than the closed air that brought with it the scent of must and old decaying things. A welcome breeze blew through the window relieving the stifling heat.

Jen glanced around. She focused her flashlight in a dark corner and was rewarded with the sight of a trunk she hadn't noticed before. The floorboards creaked as she approached. Objects in the trunk had been carefully sequestered. Folded in yellowed sheeting she found a man's military uniform. Not a recent uniform. In fact, it looked to be a Union officer's clothing from the Civil War period. She found a photo, a very old one. The man in the photo wore what she thought appeared to be the uniform in the trunk. She looked further and located a packet of letters. The letters were from a Colonel Charles Pritchard to his wife Amelia. Jen would read them when she could. The writing was faded and the yellowed paper itself fragile. She handled them with utmost delicacy. Digging down further, she located something heavy. What could it be?

She lifted the wrapped object out of the trunk with some effort. Uncovering the cloth, she could see it was a scabbard and inside of that was a sword. The hilt was black. She brought it over to the window to get a better look. The hilt was made of solid silver which had oxidized. She would clean it. Carefully she removed the sword from the scabbard and viewed the blade. It had been forged from steel. It must have been part of Charles Pritchard's dress uniform. How lovely it would be to display these things. They were part of American history, certainly part of her family history. Aaron would be so excited. What an amazing find! She would leave it in front of the trunk for the time being and show it to Aaron later today, but warn him not to touch the blade itself.

Jen looked around some more and located more clothing from other eras, although nothing as impressive as the wedding dress she and Maryann had previously found. A Tiffany lamp with a crack in the shade interested her. She wondered if such an object could be restored. Soon it became too hot to continue working in the attic. She put the attic fan on again after she dusted, removed some debris and went back downstairs where it felt much cooler. She felt jazzed about her unexpected finds.

Jen decided to take the Civil War letters of Charles Pritchard out to the backyard and sit in the shade to read them where the light seemed best. She settled herself on the chaise under a large oak tree, excited and eager to examine the letters.

She could not completely decipher his words, but what she could read convinced Jen the letters had historical significance. Charles spoke of skirmishes as well as famous battles. However, the warmth of the day and her physical efforts in the attic had tired her. Soon her eyelids were drooping.

Jen came awake with a start. She hadn't realized she'd fallen asleep but the letters she'd been reading were on the ground. A shadow fell across her. She blinked, looked up at a man in a black ski mask, and started to scream. A gloved hand smothered the sound. The man, dressed all in black clothing, presented a sinister image like a ninja in an action move, except this was no film, but instead real life horror.

A hand painfully gripped her arm forcing her to her feet. She felt something metallic shoved into her side.

"Don't try to speak or I'll shoot you here. Do you understand?" The voice insinuated itself into her ear.

When she didn't respond, the man pushed his weapon harder. She cringed in pain and nodded.

"All right. That's better. We're going into the house now." He removed his hand from her mouth.

"There's a camera. They'll know you're here. They'll see you and send someone."

He laughed, an ugly sound that chilled her to the marrow in spite of the heat of the day.

"I'm not stupid. I took care of disabling the camera during the night. I've been watching you through binoculars from the woods. I see you come and sit out here every day. So predictable. So stupid."

Jen had been foolish, she realized. The back of the house had woodland behind it and no direct neighbors. No one could see what was happening. The house had a lot of privacy. That had its benefits. But at the moment it proved a detriment. The hedges were high and the neighbors weren't close on either side. The Pritchard house had land, maybe too much of it.

The intruder forced her in through the back of the house up the side stairs into the kitchen area. He pulled off his mask and Jen found herself staring into the face of Edward Norris.

"If you try to kill me again, they'll know you're responsible."

He laughed. "No they won't. It will look like a burglar entered and murdered you. This weapon can't be traced. I'm wearing gloves. No fingerprints."

"No alibi."

"Wrong. My wife will testify I worked in my study all morning. I left through a rear window and will return the same say."

"It doesn't matter. Chief Coleman will know. He'll be relentless."

Norris gave her a smug look. "He won't be able to prove anything. My lawyer explained you're the only witness who can testify I tried to kill you. With you dead, there's no case. And the charities will receive what remains from your grandmother's estate. I'll make some restitution and be out of jail in a year or two. Maybe I won't serve any prison time at all. My lawyer is excellent. Worth every cent I'll be forced to pay the bloodsucker."

Norris, wild-eyed and red-faced, frightened her. Jen's mouth felt dry. How could she deal with this mentally unbalanced man? He would shoot her in moments. She must think of something to stop him. But what?

Desperate, she glanced around. He threw her a knowing look. "No one can save you." He raised the gun he held. "You'll die, just like the old lady did."

"You murdered my grandmother?"

"She proved easier to kill than you have. All I had to do was visit her room in the middle of the night and press a pillow over her face."

"You're a monster!"

He bared his teeth. "My uncle said she was feeling better, asking for an accounting of her assets and investments. Of course, she had to die. And so will you."

Jen yanked her arm free of his grasp. Looking down at the kitchen table, she saw the glass of orange juice left over from breakfast that morning. She grasped it in her hand and threw it into his eyes. Then she snatched up her cell phone and ran.

Norris gasped. Caught off-guard for a moment, he rubbed the juice from his eyes. Jen was already running toward the stairs. She wanted to get to her room and lock the door so she could phone the police. Thankfully, she had her cell phone in hand. A land line was also located in her bedroom.

Unfortunately, Norris was quick. He tried to grasp her arm again.

Jen was alert now and able to move out of his vicinity, running up the stairs with speed released by an adrenalin rush. Norris got off a shot which went wild and hit the wall behind her. Butterflies screamed in her stomach. Jen was frantic. She realized if she went to her bedroom he would be able to shoot her in the back before she could even enter. She needed some advantage or she would be dead in moments.

She kept on running. There might be a way. A slim chance. But even a slim chance would be better than none. She ran to the stairs which led to the attic. He'd gotten off another shot by then. Thank God his aim at a moving target wasn't all that good. She wouldn't stop, would not give him an opportunity to kill her easily.

Jen made it into the attic, her chest heaving, near collapse, barely able to draw another breath. The door didn't have a lock. Still, she did manage to shove a heavy chest against it. She tried to dial 911, but the door came crashing open before she could complete the call. She hid in the darkest corner by the chest where she'd found the Civil War memorabilia.

"Come out! You can't escape."

Jen opened the scabbard and removed the sword. It wasn't easy because her palms were sweating so. She could barely grip the hilt even using both hands. God, it was so heavy!

Grant sat at his desk writing yet another annoying report. His telephone rang and he admitted to himself that he felt glad for the interruption.

"Coleman here."

"Yeah, Grant, this is your favorite brother."

"And my only brother." Grant smiled.

"Right. Now that we've handled the pleasantries, I want to mention something to you."

"Shoot."

"I'd rather you didn't. Well, anyhow this probably doesn't mean anything, but it's been niggling in my mind."

"What has?"

"Jen Stoddard asked me to find out for her about installing a burglar alarm system."

"Good idea under the circumstances."

"Right. Well, I contacted a couple of reliable companies, but as you know they're not local. Let's face it, there's not much call for burglar alarms in a town like Bloomingvale. Anyhow, the earliest anyone can do the job is the beginning of next week."

"And you let Jen know that?"

Rob hesitated at his end. "That's the thing. I tried calling her this morning a bunch of times."

"She's probably out."

"Yeah, but she should have at least answered her cell. I've done a lot of work for the lady and she's very responsible. It's not like her. Maybe it's nothing, but with that creep Norris out on bail, I got to thinking maybe someone ought to check on her. I'm out on a job right now and can't do it myself."

"No problem. I can be over there in a few minutes."

Grant got going. He left his destination information with the dispatcher and hurried out. Probably there would be nothing wrong when he got to the Pritchard house but his brother happened to be right. Point taken. Better safe than sorry as the old saying went.

Chapter Fifty-Two

"I know you're in that corner. I hear you breathing You can't hide from me. I'll shoot you if you don't come out here." He'd shoot her regardless. She was certain of it.

Jen didn't speak. She held her grip tight on the sword.

"Get out here now!" He sounded demented, out of control.

Jen cringed and scrunched down further in her dark corner.

Norris let go of two more rounds. Neither one touched her. However, Jen knew it would be just a matter of time before he succeeded in shooting her.

"I'm right here," she said, letting him hear her voice. "If you want me, you'll have to come for me."

She heard his heavy tread moving toward her corner. She thought her heart would surely burst. But with every bit of strength she possessed, using both hands, Jen slashed at Edward Norris. She must have caught his legs because he screamed.

She rose from her crouched position and moved swiftly toward the attic door. She heard him breathing hard right behind her.

"You're dead!" he shouted.

She swallowed hard, expecting to be shot dead in a matter of seconds. But she kept moving.

"Stop! Drop that!" Jen did neither.

All of a sudden, the door burst open. Grant Coleman stood there, gun drawn.

"Slow and easy, Norris. Put your weapon on the floor and walk away. Then place your hands behind your head. Jen get over here by me."

Norris tried to make a grab for Jen, reaching for her with his free hand. She had no intention of allowing that to happen. She brought down the blade of the sword on his hand. Norris shouted out his pain and then brought his gun around to shoot her. Jen cringed as a shot rang out. But Norris took a bullet, not her. The force of Grant's gun blast caused Norris to lose his balance, stagger, and fall backward through the still open attic window.

"Are you all right?"

She dropped the sword and rushed into Grant's arms. She found herself sobbing and shaking at the same time, and couldn't control either reaction. Grant shushed her, held her tight, kissing her cheeks.

"He tried to kill me again. I can't believe you came. You saved me."

He rubbed her back in a soothing manner. "You really saved yourself. You're an incredibly brave woman."

Grant let go of her and walked over to the window. He looked down. "I'm fairly certain Norris is dead."

Grant took her back in his arms and kissed her deeply, passionately. Jen returned his kiss with intense hunger and longing. His strong arms made her feel comforted, as if she'd finally and truly come home.

Jen phoned Maryann on the following day and told her what had happened. She found herself still reacting to the trauma. Her voice sounded thread even to her own ears.

"What a horror show. Are you okay?"

"Better now. I'm just so glad that it didn't happen when Aaron was here."

"Aaron was at school?"

"Yes. And when I called Maggie Higgins and explained, she picked the children up from school and brought Aaron to her house. She kept him there until everything was taken care of. "

"I wish I could have been there to help you."

"I doubt there was much you could have done."

"You're really handling this well, Jen."

"Thanks for saying that. Inside I'm still quivering like jelly. I forgot to ask how your interviews went."

"I'm going to tell you all about it–in person."

"You're coming back here?"

"Don't sound so surprised."

"Of course I'm surprised. How could I not be? Is it because of what happened to me?"

"No, it's not."

"All right. But when are you returning?"

"I'll let you know. It will be soon though."

"Aaron will be thrilled. So will Rob."

"I'm not certain how Rob is going to react. We'll see about that."

"Will you phone him?"

"We'll see."

Maryann ended the phone call, Clearly not wanting to say more to her for the time being.

Jen stared at the phone after her call from Maryann ended. The conversation had been a peculiar one. But Jen felt too fatigued to dwell upon it.

Jen looked at the time. Ten in the morning. She fixed herself a cup of coffee and sat down at the kitchen table trying to sort out her thoughts and emotions. So much had happened to her since returning to town.

The doorbell rang. Jen jumped to her feet her nerves still jangling. She pulled back the curtain at one side of the glass windows that bordered the front entrance. Grant stood there and she immediately opened the door to allow him to enter.

"I hope I'm not disturbing you," he said. "I just came by to make certain that you're okay."

"I am, more or less. Can I offer you a cup of coffee?"

"Sure."

"I could bring it to you in the living room."

"Kitchen's fine for me."

He followed her out. She was glad now that she'd brewed a pot, although she rarely drank more than one cup of coffee a day, if that, and so generally drank instant coffee. She poured him a cup and placed some of Aaron's favorite chocolate chip cookies on a plate.

"Cream, milk, sugar?"

"Just black is fine."

She sat down opposite him. "I'm glad you came by."

"Are you?" He looked up at her, wrinkling his long forehead.

"Yes, very glad."

He lifted a cookie and turned it around in his hand. "I want to ask you something that's been bothering me."

"Sure, anything."

"You said that you forgave me. And I got annoyed. What exactly were you forgiving me for?"

Jen felt her face flush. "Of course, you wouldn't know, wouldn't even remember. I was foolish to say anything. I never meant to say a word about it."

He broke the cookie in half. "Tell me. I want to know what you were talking about." His eyes met hers. They were sharp and metallic now.

Jen looked away. "It's silly really."

"Tell me." She sat down opposite him, pulling her hand away. "Fine. Back in high school we worked on that Shakespeare project together. You asked me out and I accepted. Then you stood me up."

"I what?" He rose to his feet.

"You didn't show up at my parents' house that Saturday night. You didn't call. You never even apologized. I guess you probably forgot you ever asked me. You were so very popular, and I was just some nerd who had no real friends."

He stared at her and then shook his head. "You're talking about our senior year of high school?"

"Correct."

"That is not at all what happened."

"It isn't?"

"No, it's not." He stood up abruptly practically knocking over his coffee cup.

Jen got to her feet, hands on her hips and faced him. "Why don't you explain what happened then? I'd love to know. I felt crushed. I was crazy about you."

"You were? I didn't know that. I came to your house that night. I didn't forget our date."

Jen stared at him in bewilderment. "I don't understand. My mother told me to wait in my room until she called me, that when you arrived, she'd let me know. I spent ages trying on different outfits. But my mother never called me to come downstairs. When I checked the time and discovered it was eight-thirty, a half hour later than you were expected, I did come down. My mother said you never arrived. I waited and waited in the living room. Finally, at ten o'clock, I went back to my room and spent the night crying."

Grant reached out and pulled her into his arms. "Jen, I was there. In fact, I came early, before eight in the evening. I guess your mother had been waiting for me because I never even got to ring the doorbell. She came outside and spoke to me on your porch."

"What did she say?"

"That you'd changed your mind. You didn't want to go out with me. She said that you'd found out about my father being a drunk, that my mother worked as a cleaning lady for your grandmother, and you realized I was trash."

Jen felt shocked. "She actually said those things to you?"

"They're etched in my memory as if it were yesterday."

Jen felt tears well up in her eyes. "You shouldn't have believed her."

"Your mother was very convincing."

Jen took his face in her hands, reaching upward. "Please believe me when I say I never thought or expressed such terrible things. I thought that you rejected me. I understood it but still felt crushed."

Grant placed his arms around her and held her close. "I felt the same way about you."

"Can we start over again, please?"

"I'd like that very much."

He kissed her and she kissed him back with all the love she now felt for him.

"I want to make love to you," he whispered. "But it can wait until you're feeling better."

Chapter Fifty-Three

Maryann waited at the airport for Jen to pick her up. She glanced at her watch. The plane landed on time, but her friend must have been running late.

"Looking for somebody?" The familiar deep voice wasn't the one she expected.

"Rob, what are you doing here?"

"Came to pick you up. Jen couldn't make it. Aaron got sent home from school sick. She had to pick him up and take him over to the doc's office."

"I hope he's all right." She felt concerned. Aaron tended to be healthy and both she and Jen had taken that for granted.

"There's something going around. I think the school nurse thought he needed a strep culture."

"I'm sorry to have inconvenienced you like this."

"Let's get your stuff." He didn't comment when he saw all of her luggage. But as he loaded the bags into the back of his pick-up truck and frowned at her.

"Didn't find a job?" His T-shirt clung to his glistening muscles.

"Actually, I was offered two very good positions." She lifted her chin.

"Then why are you here?"

"I intend to discuss my change of plans with Jen first."

"All right." He gave her a curt nod.

Jen welcomed Maryann with open arms on the porch of her house. They hugged as Rob Coleman brought Maryann's baggage up the stairs and into the house.

"How's Aaron?"

"Better now. The doctor did a culture. In the meantime, I gave him some medicine for the fever and he's resting upstairs. Several of the children in his class are also sick."

"Jen, if it's a problem for me to stay here right now, just let me know. I can stay at the inn or at a motel."

"No problem at all, unless you mind being exposed to a sick child."

"I think I had everything when I was little. I'm not worried about that."

Rob joined them on the porch. "All your stuff's in the front hall. I guess you'll take it from there. I better get back on the job." She noticed the scowl he turned on Maryann and wondered at it.

Jen hugged him. "Rob, thanks so much for your help and for being such a good friend."

"Not a problem." He turned to Maryann. "So I guess I'll see you around."

"I guess you will."

Rob left without further comment. Maryann watched him leave, her expression thoughtful. Jen decided not to push her friend for information.

"So why don't we get something to drink? Are you hungry? When did you eat last?"

"I'm okay. But I do have some things I want to talk over with you."

"Sure, let's go out to the kitchen and have some cold drinks."

Jen fixed them both iced tea plus avocado and tomato sandwiches on whole grain bread.

"So what's up? Why are you back here so soon? I thought you'd be busy in the city."

"Jen, when I got back to the city, I had this sense of wrongness, like I didn't belong there anymore. It was so weird. I thought it would pass. After all, I'd been out of town for a month. But then I went for the job interviews. The first job I interviewed for was with an ad agency. The position paid well but in return for slave labor. The second job where I interviewed and received an offer was at a pharma firm. I would have to travel two weeks out of every month. The woman I interviewed with explained what a great opportunity it was. All I could think of was that my whole life would be my job and they could let me go again whenever they chose to downsize or close down the department. I started wondering if there couldn't be more to life than that."

Jen listened thoughtfully to Maryann. "You were let go in spite of the fact you worked hard for the company and did a great job for them. You devoted your life to the corporation and your job. You gave them your complete loyalty and devotion, and so you felt betrayed and disillusioned. I understand."

"Rob was the one who started me thinking, wondering if maybe I should make changes in my life. Anyway, I went to visit my parents. Do you know I hadn't seen them since Christmas? I wouldn't have even gone then but for the fact that you were visiting Bill's parents so they could spend time with their grandson for the holidays, and I didn't want to spend the holiday alone."

"I'm certain your folks were happy to see you again."

"I suppose." Maryann took another sip of her drink. Her expression remained solemn.

"Jen, I asked them for money, not a gift though. I asked for a loan to be paid back with interest."

Jen raised her dark auburn eyebrows. "Money to pay back your student loans?"

"Partly. I've been thinking about that empty shop between the bookstore and the bakery that you and I looked at."

Jen smiled. "Funny, I've been thinking about it too."

"I've been thinking it's a good location for an antique shop."

She brought her hand to her chin. "That's an interesting idea."

"I have enough money to rent and renovate the shop. I know you can't sell anything in this house, but maybe we could put some of the interesting things on display, like that Victorian wedding dress."

"Or the Civil War memorabilia I found."

"Exactly. I was thinking we could take antiques on consignment. If they sell, we take a percentage. If they don't sell, after a certain amount of time, we return that particular consignment to the owner. I would handle the marketing and promotion end. We could work weekends together and change off hours during the week. What do you think? Admittedly, the plan's a bit rough right now. You might have some suggestions."

Jen rose to her feet. "I'm excited. I think it's a wonderful idea. Do you still want to sell coffee?"

Maryann put her forefinger to her lips. "I thought about it. I wouldn't want any coffee spills on valuable antiques or period costumes. I'm tempted to offer to manage the bakery if the Bigelows are serious about moving to Florida. I believe the display cases could be moved around so that there would be room to place tables and chairs by the front window. Coffee urns could be brought in and people would be able to enjoy pastries along with their beverages. Could be a good money-making proposition. Also, I think there are some possibilities for the bookstore, like making it have a friendlier, cozier place by placing comfortable chairs by the front windows."

"But no food or beverages there?"

"No, none at all. Just attractive book and magazine displays. Maybe selling some tech stuff as well. I don't have all of that worked out yet."

"You'd consider managing three stores?" Jen shook her head. "You are ambitious."

"Don't forget hardworking."

Jen laughed. "That too."

"So what do you think?"

"I love it. I've been at loose ends here, not knowing what to do with myself when Aaron's in school. I'd really love to work."

"Well, you know I'd put all my efforts into it plus all the money my parents loaned me. But I would need to live here at least in the beginning. Would that be okay?"

"Of course," Jen said. Her conscience troubled her. She realized Maryann ought to be told about the money she had found.

"Maryann, I located a note from my grandmother in her room. She had a wall safe. She left me a nice amount of cash in an envelope that I can now put into the business. So it's not all going to be weighing on your shoulders. We can go in as equal partners in the antique business. We'll read up on it too. I can't think of anything more interesting."

Maryann stood up and shook Jen's hand. "Partners."

"You bet."

"We'll roll the dice together," Maryann said.

"It won't be that much of a gamble," Jen said. "I have a good feeling about this. We'll make a go of it."

Chapter Fifty-Four

Grant fixed a steely eyed look on him. "Rob, you mean to tell me you picked her up at the airport and you hardly spoke to each other?"

Rob sucked the ice from his soda. "You got it."

Grant shook his head. "I don't understand. You tell me you're crazy in love with the girl, but now you're angry at her, won't event talk to her."

They'd taken a booth in the diner in the back corner. Since lunch had long since finished and dinner wouldn't be served for two more hours, they pretty much had the place to themselves.

After dropping Maryann at the Pritchard house, Rob had gone back on the job to the house he and his crew were currently renovating. But everything seemed under control. They didn't need him at the moment. He felt too frustrated to work right now anyway. Maryann had crawled under his skin. So he phoned Grant and asked if they could meet for a little while. The diner seemed like neutral ground.

But Grant hadn't been showing him the kind of sympathy or understanding he would have expected.

"Aren't you going to tell me how she and Jen Stoddard are snobs and I shouldn't have anything to do with Maryann?"

Grant lowered his eyes. "I could have been wrong about that."

Rob stared at his brother. "You changed your mind about them?"

"Well, about Jen anyway. You could say that we had a misunderstanding back in the day. Didn't happen to be my fault or·hers. I feel like we lost a lot of time together. Can't make up for it, but I can right things now. Don't let that happen to you. Maybe Maryann's waiting for you to say something to her. She came back, didn't she? Brought all that luggage with her? Doesn't that count for something?"

Rob left the diner realizing he had a lot to consider. What Grant said made sense. Still, he couldn't be certain of Maryann's feelings. He drove back to the Pritchard house, hoping he wasn't making a mistake.

Jen let him in before he could even ring the bell or knock. "We saw you drive up. Aaron's still asleep so we're trying to keep quiet. I'm so glad you came back. We were going to phone you this evening."

"We?"

Jen hooked his arm and led him into the living room. Maryann sat on a rocking chair talking on her cell phone. She looked up at him.

"Mom, I've got to go. Just wanted you and Dad to know that I arrived safely. I'll phone again soon and let you know how things are going here." She put the phone down on an end table.

"Well, Mary, Mary quite contrary, are you ready to tell me how your garden grows?"

"Humph." She narrowed her gaze.

"What does that mean?"

"That I haven't liked the tone you've taken toward me."

He took her hand and pulled her to her feet. Then he sat her down beside him on the closer of the two sofas. "Okay, no more dancing around. Time for some serious conversation."

"Excuse me," Jen said. "I have to check on Aaron." She hurried from the room.

"Now see, I think you made her feel uncomfortable, and in her own home at that."

He didn't let go of her hand. "You exasperate me, lady. You know that?"

She shrugged. "It's not intentional."

"I think it is. Now tell me straight out what's going on."

She did and he listened with total interest.

"Wow! You sure got some ambitious plans." He ran his hands through his hair.

She smiled at him, making him think of sunshine as her hair caught the glow of the late afternoon sun through the window.

"I think the business will work. I'm not afraid of hard work. That's something we have in common."

He thought what a joy she was to look at and how he'd find the utmost pleasure in looking at her for the rest of his life.

"Jen and I will want to hire you to renovate our store. We know how good you are."

"I'd consider it an honor and a privilege. But why are you doing this? Why didn't you stay in New York? I thought that was what you wanted."

She lowered her gaze. "I thought it was too. But I realized I was wrong. Your words kept running through my mind, haunting me. I realize that I've changed. And it's all your fault." She pointed an accusing finger at him.

"What did I do?"

"You made me question myself. You made me want more than just work. You made me see that I needed a more complete existence. I don't want to spend my life alone anymore."

That was all he needed to hear. Rob took Maryann in his arms and kissed her. She looped her arms around his neck and drew closer to him, returning his kiss with enthusiasm. He felt swamped with emotion, dazed and dazzled by her. His lips skimmed her cheeks, her chin, and then the swanlike curve of her throat.

"I love you so much," he said. "I'm going to ask you again. Will you marry me?"

"Yes, I love you too. I didn't recognize how much until I left here. But I honestly didn't think you'd still want me after I refused you before."

"But you came back anyway."

She nodded and there were tears in her great green eyes. "I felt bereft. I hoped there might still be a chance for us."

He caressed her cheek. "We'll get married as soon as I finish building the house for us. You pick out everything you want to see in it."

"I'll be frugal."

"Honey, business is good. Gonna build you a fine house, worthy of my bride."

They kissed again, holding nothing back.

Chapter Fifty-five

The Coleman clan gathered in her grandmother's dining room. Jen had invited Rob's family to a celebratory dinner. Rob and Maryann had officially announced their engagement. Maryann flashed her blue white diamond ring for everyone to see. Lori grabbed Maryann's hand to get a better look.

"Oh, it's so beautiful," Sue gushed. "Rob, you have such good taste in jewelry. What a surprise."

He offered a modest shrug. "Maryann chose the stone and the setting. I just paid for it."

"The most important part," Linda assured him with a big smile. "So Maryann, Rob tells us that you are going to manage our local bookstore and possibly the bakery. You and Jennifer are going to be partners in an antique business besides. I admire your energy and drive."

"Rob's encouraged me to take chances. I think the three shops together will offer shoppers a special enjoyable experience."

Jen turned to the others, sweeping her gaze over the group as a whole. "Maryann came up with a great name for the shop: Everything Old Is New Again. What do you think?"

"Clever," Grant said with an approving nod. "I like it."

"So do I," Rob agreed, placing a supportive arm around Maryann.

The doorbell rang. "Are we expecting more company?" Maryann turned an inquiring look on Jen.

"Did you ask Bobby?" Aaron jumped up. "I'll get it."

"I didn't invite the Higgins family," Jen called after him. "Excuse me." She went after her son.

When she reached the front door, Jen observed her son staring at a woman who he did not know.

He remained in the doorway. "Mom, this lady says she's my grandmother. But how can she be?"

Jen placed her hand on her bewildered son's shoulder. "Aaron, this is Grandma Sara, my mother. She is your grandmother. You have two grandmothers. You just haven't seen Grandma Sara since you were very little."

"Sorry," he said to Jen's mother. "I don't remember you."

"I wouldn't expect it." Sara Morrow gave Jen a critical look.

"Would you like to come in and join us for dinner?"

"Why did you extend the invitation?" Sara sniffed the air and narrowed her eyes as if suspicious.

"Aaron, would you please tell our guests that I'll be returning in a few minutes to serve the main course."

He skipped away.

"I don't want to keep you from your guests."

"You're welcome to stay and break bread with us. My friend Maryann has gotten engaged to Rob Coleman. I believe you are acquainted with Linda Coleman and her son Grant. I invited Rob's family to dinner to celebrate the engagement. That's why I left the message at your motel. I thought you might want to come as well. It's a good opportunity for you to get to know Aaron."

Sara opened her mouth but then closed it again.

"What's the matter, Mother?"

"Linda Coleman is a cleaning lady. She worked for your grandmother. She and her children aren't the sort of people who should be guests in this house."

"I believe you told Grant something of the sort when we were in high school." Jen made an effort not to raise her voice or sound accusatory. She knew having dealt with her mother over the years that it would do no good at all. "I discovered that all those years ago you lied to me and you lied to Grant. It was an incredibly cruel thing to do. How could you?"

"I protected you. You happened to be a minor, my responsibility."

Jen shook her head. "I'm sorry. I don't believe that. However, I believe in doing unto others as I would have them

216

do unto me. So I invited you to my home today for dinner in spite of our differences."

"Ha, you are doing this to insult me. Admit it! I thought you left that message for me because you realized that I should share in your grandmother's estate with you."

"I thought about that and I agree. I will share whatever money there is when the reckoning is made in two years. You can have your lawyer draw up an agreement to that effect. I'll sign it."

"You will?" Her mother looked jubilant.

"That's right. You don't need to drag this matter through the courts with an expensive law suit that you'll ultimately lose anyway. You can have half of the remaining assets, outside of the house itself which I intend to continue living in and the furnishings which I hope to restore."

Her mother's small eyes moved around. Her expression appeared thoughtful. "All right, I agree. I don't want the house anyway. You're welcome to it and good riddance. As for me, I'm going back to Chicago. Frank and I split up, but the city's full of lively people. Thank goodness your father still provides me with alimony so I can live decently."

"As I said, you're welcome to stay for dinner."

"Some other time maybe."

Jen closed the front door as her mother walked out.

"She gone?" Grant joined her.

Jen managed a nod. "Did Aaron tell you she came?"

"If you want to keep a secret, don't tell your son." He gave her a wry smile.

"It wasn't a secret. I extended an olive branch to her."

Grant's expression darkened. "Why would you do that?"

"She's a horrible person, but she is still my mother. I made a decision to share my grandmother's inheritance with her when I receive it. I wanted to let her know. There's been enough unpleasantness. I want it to end. I'm also going to donate funds to each of the charities my Grandmother gave money to, except for the Forrest Foundation."

Grant took her in his arms. "You're a mighty decent human being."

She looked up at him and smiled. "Some would say foolish."

He kissed her forehead. "I wouldn't be one of them."

She closed her eyes and felt his breath inches from her own. Then he kissed her lips. She lifted her arms and caressed the back of his neck, kissing him back.

"We lost a lot of time," he said. "It pains me to think about it."

Jen shook her head. She realized that her years with Bill had been good ones until the end of his life when they had suffered horribly. But she wouldn't trade any of those years because she had a wonderful son.

"I love you," Grant said. "We are meant to be together, to share our lives. I want to marry you. And I like Aaron. He's a good kid. I wouldn't try to replace his father, but there are lots of things we could do together." That brought joy to her heart.

His steady gaze met hers as he held her hands in his.

"How would you feel about having a kid with me?"

"I can't think of anything that would make me happier."

As he kissed her again, Jen knew it was true. She realized this was what her grandmother had wanted for her. She had finally and truly come home.

ABOUT THE AUTHOR

Multiple award-winning author, Jacqueline Seewald, has taught creative, expository and technical writing at Rutgers University as well as high school English.

She also worked as both an academic librarian and an educational media specialist. Sixteen of her books of fiction have been published to critical praise including books for adults, teens and children.

Her short stories, poems, essays, reviews and articles have appeared in hundreds of diverse publications and numerous anthologies such as: *The Writer, L.A. Times, Reader's Digest, Pedestal, Sherlock Holmes Mystery Magazine, Over My Dead Body!, Gumshoe Review, The Mystery Megapack, and The Christian Science Monitor*.

She's also an amateur landscape artist and loves blue grass music. She loves hearing from readers. Her writer's blog can be found at:
http://jacquelineseewald.blogspot.com